Sound of Silence

"*Sound of Silence* is Young Adult writing at its finest. With little to no sex on the page and a story that will hit home for so many teenagers, the beauty that rises from the ashes of these three broken lives is stunning."
—Joyfully Jay

"…together these authors have created what is surely going to be one of my favourite books this year."
—Love Bytes

Us Three

"This is a must read, guys, especially if you're looking for a story about finding true love in the oddest of places and not only standing up for yourself, but what is right and the people you love."
—MM Good Book Reviews

"It's a rollercoaster, it's filled with pitfalls and hellish situations, but it's also full of love and family, and three amazing young men of whom, by the end of the book, I was immensely proud."
—My Fiction Nook

The Red Sheet

"*The Red Sheet* had me in awe from beginning to end. Honestly, I don't feel worthy to review it; I just hope I can do it justice."
—Prism Book Alliance

"This book had me from the word go. One of the best Young Adult books I've read."
—The Tipsy Bibliophile

By MIA KERICK

Intervention
My Crunchy Life
Not Broken, Just Bent
The Princess of Baker Street
The Red Sheet
With Raine O'Tierney: Sound of Silence

ONE VOICE
Us Three

Published by HARMONY INK PRESS
www.harmonyinkpress.com

The Princess of Baker Street

MIA KERICK

Harmony Ink

Published by

HARMONY INK PRESS

5032 Capital Circle SW, Suite 2, PMB# 279, Tallahassee, FL 32305-7886 USA
publisher@harmonyinkpress.com • harmonyinkpress.com

This is a work of fiction. Names, characters, places, and incidents either are the product of author imagination or are used fictitiously, and any resemblance to actual persons, living or dead, business establishments, events, or locales is entirely coincidental.

The Princess of Baker Street
© 2019 Mia Kerick.

Cover Art
© 2019 Tiferet Design.
http://www.tiferetdesign.com/.
Cover content is for illustrative purposes only and any person depicted on the cover is a model.

Trade Paperback ISBN: 978-1-64080-395-4
Digital ISBN: 978-1-64080-394-7
Library of Congress Control Number: 2018904471
Trade Paperback published January 2019
v. 1.0

Printed in the United States of America
∞
This paper meets the requirements of
ANSI/NISO Z39.48-1992 (Permanence of Paper).

PART I
Lip gloss, Leggings, and a Scarf

1

TRAVIS JENKINS and me lean against the oak tree on the corner at the Baker Street bus stop. Leaning makes us look way cooler than just standing would.

"I found your math book underneath a bus seat yesterday afternoon, Eric. How'd you get your homework done last night, huh?" Emily Monterey has morphed into a second mother. Like I need another mom.

I tug on my left earlobe. It hurts worse than the time I fell off my skateboard riding down the stairs in front of the library and rammed my front teeth through my bottom lip. Ever since Lily Lee pierced it with an ice cube and a needle on Saturday afternoon, it's never been right. If it doesn't quit swelling up, I'm going to pull the goddamned golden hoop out—it makes me look more like a pirate than a gangsta anyhow.

"Maybe I didn't do the friggin' math homework—*so sue me*." I know how to sound meaner than my backyard neighbor's dog when I hang out too close to the fence. But Emily is sensitive when it comes to backtalk; even though I snap at her so she'll chill with the lecturing, I wink so she doesn't have a meltdown.

The wink works *too* good—Emily keeps right on yapping. "Mark my words, Eric, you're *so* going to get another detention for not passing it in."

She points this out like I don't already know how shit works with Mr. Carr. What Emily doesn't know is I wouldn't have a clue how to do the math problems even if I *had* my math book. Maybe I forgot it on the bus accidentally on purpose.

"Whatever," I say, and I yawn so nobody thinks I give a shit if I flunk out. Then I step right up behind the girls who're standing on the sidewalk next to the Kinkaids' fancy painted mailbox. I unzip Emily's backpack and pull out my math book, even though I wish it had disappeared like anything good I ever left on the bus did before—like my headphones and my baseball glove.

And right now it's as if my eyes got minds all their own. They *make* me look past Emily and up the walkway at the huge yellow house, and at Joey. As usual his butt is planted on his front doorstep, and, as usual, he's got his nose stuck in a book. Joey Kinkaid, the genius of the eighth grade, could've helped me figure out how to do my math problems last night, and I know this for a fact because I know Joey like I know too-hot pizza will burn the skin off the roof of my mouth and make it tingle for three days.

Why can't I turn off my brain when the memories of how it used to be with the Baker Street kids and Joey start playing like a movie in my head?

"Chase me!" Joey yells, and Emily and Travis and Lily and me run after him down Baker Street. We all make fish faces and wave our arms around 'cause Joey says we're really sea creatures swimming in the ocean.

Like always Emily runs too close on Joey's heels. All I can do is hold my breath and wait for her to give him a flat tire, and like always, it makes Joey trip on his dress and fall flat on his face. After me and Travis help him up and dust the pebbles off his knees, Emily shouts, "Don't blame me—I can't help it I run up the back of Joey's legs! I run the fastest 'cause I'm the only one who's already turned seven around here!"

I think Em's just mad 'cause she never gets to be the Little Mermaid.

When we used to chase Joey around the neighborhood, he'd start singing about how he wanted to be part of our world, and it was like he almost *turned into* Princess Ariel for real. It made me forget he was Joey—I really thought he was the girl who had everything.

I can't be daydreaming in public about how Joey was our princess, so I shake my head a couple of times. When my mind comes back to the real world at the Baker Street bus stop, Travis is giving him crap. "Hey, Josie! Whatcha reading?" When Travis calls him Josie, it twists me up inside.

Joey glances up from his paperback book and tilts his head, so there's no doubt he heard Travis's question. A whoosh of breath gushes out of my mouth, and I hope Travis doesn't hear because he'll say I care. And I *can't* care about Joey anymore, but I also can't miss that he's still as pretty as he was when we were kids and hung out together every day after school, except for Tuesdays, when he had clarinet lessons. Back then his light-blond hair fell loose and scraggly around his shoulders, but now he wears it combed real neat and held back with a soft black hairband. Somehow that velvety band pulling his hair off his face makes his eyes and nose look round and cute and innocent, like a baby seal's in a *National Geographic* magazine... and his lips are so damned pink. There's no other way to slice it—Joey looks more like somebody's sweet little sister than ever, even if he's thirteen now and wears nerdy boys' clothes instead of his mom's dress.

"Answer me, Kinkaid!" Travis demands, his eyes bulging and his face turning red. If Joey wasn't sitting on his doorstep, and if we all didn't know his mom was watching out the window like his guardian angel, Travis would be up in Joey's face. "Answer me, or I'm gonna make you eat dirt!"

"Why do you care so much 'bout what he's reading?" I ask Travis, but my voice comes out sounding too high and shaky for my own safety. Everybody knows when you're calling another kid out, you got to sound like you got balls. Lily gawks at me like I'm from Pluto—and it's not even a planet anymore—because

Travis has grown to be the biggest dude in the whole eighth grade by a mile, and nobody messes with him. He's as strong as The Rock, and worse, he's a hothead—like "punch first, think later" is his life's motto. But I've known him longer than anybody else in Wild Acres, and once in a while, he still listens to me.

Not this time, though—Travis is pissed off at me now. He grabs me by my third-day-of-school new white T-shirt and shoves me backward, hard. I live ready for moments like this, so I don't stumble, but I already know I'm not going to push my luck anymore. "Maybe I wanna know what a genius reads when he's hiding on his doorstep like a big wuss." He squawks a couple times like a chicken. "What's it to you anyhow, Sinclair?"

"It's nothing." I don't spend too much time defending Joey from the entire student body of Wild Acres Middle School anymore. Back in seventh grade, I used to try to look out for him sometimes, but it didn't take long until I figured out it was a total waste of energy. On a Monday I could tell everybody "Joey's *not* a princess" until I was blue in the face, and then on Tuesday he'd show up at school wearing nail polish and a charm bracelet, and he'd be the princess of the middle school again. Mom always says, "God helps those who help themselves," and since Joey Kinkaid isn't doing himself any favors, why the hell should I?

Too bad I can't forget what a perfect kind of princess Joey made when we played together on Baker Street....

"I am going to swim up to the surface now." Princess Ariel says it like she's a teacher giving directions to the orange group—loud and clear and slow—and I know it's time for me to be Prince Eric and fall off the boat and start drowning. I crawl about halfway up the slide behind Lily's house and fall from there 'stead of dropping down from the very top. Mom would have my head if I broke my neck 'cause I was playing make-pretend. She'd tell me, "Trips to the ER aren't cheap, Eric." The

6

thing is, even when I fall from halfway up, it hurts like heck when I land on the ocean floor hard on my butt.

"Ooooh," I groan super loud. Princess Ariel swims over to me and smiles—she likes it that I groan when I'm drowning. She just doesn't know that sometimes I can't help it.

Back when Joey was Princess Ariel, he was so pretty and smart—sometimes he made me forget Mom's rule that kisses are for family and hugs are for friends. It was a stupid rule, anyhow. But I shiver because the truth is, if anybody else knew what I was thinking, I'd be sunk in a deep pile of crap, and I'd probably get stuck there forever.

I seriously hope there isn't a secret mind reader at the Baker Street bus stop. Nobody's looking at me funny, though, so I figure I'm safe.

Like every morning when the bus pulls up, Mrs. Kinkaid opens the front door, shouts a cheery goodbye, and then watches Joey get on like she's trying to make sure he's safe. Whether or not Joey's safe when he's stepping up onto the bus, I'm not too sure, because Travis gets a big thrill out of tripping Joey any time he gets a chance, and I think he'd get bonus points for making Joey fall out of the bus. All I know is this: if Joey *is* safe right now, it's the last time he's going to be safe all day.

Tiny goose pimples pop up all over my arms because it's so risky for Joey at school, and I'm honestly scared for him. I take the tall step onto the bus right behind him so Travis can't, and I got three things on my mind—none of them good. Number one is I'm pissed off at myself for being such a traitor to the same Joey Kinkaid I used to be best friends with. He never did anything to me. Number two is I'm worried about whether today's going to be the day I step up to the plate and defend him, killing my own chances of surviving eighth grade.

And lately number three lives in the back of my head pretty much all the time, and it's got nothing to do with Joey. I wonder if Mom will be home after school today. I haven't seen her in days, and I figure she must be wondering if I'm still alive.

Joey plunks his butt in the seat behind the driver, where he thinks he'll be safest. I plant *my* butt two seats in back of him so I can keep an eye on the kid, even though it's not my day to babysit.

2

I GOT no clue how I ended up in World Geography with a bunch of brainiacs from the grade-school blue group. It's like the school administrators were doing shots when they set up the eighth-grade class schedules on the office computers, because they messed it up royally. And I usually like to fly low under the radar, but I raise my hand because I got a question that could mean life or death to my grade.

"Excuse me, Ms. Paloma, but has there been some kind of major, like, *malfunction* with the scheduling computers, 'cause I'm not usually stuck in class with the smart kids?"

Almost everybody snickers, but I know they're wondering the same damned thing.

"No, Mr. Sinclair," Ms. Paloma replies in her I-think-I'm-God voice. "In World Geography this year—just like in the *real* world—we will be learning *together* in a *heterogeneous* group." Her tone gets sweeter, like she's going to try to sell me something. "This means that children with different levels of academic capabilities will all be cooperating to discover our wonderful world."

Oh, I get it now.

In plain words, when living and working in the *real* world, the brainiacs have got to carry the weight of the dumbasses, who have to make the brainiacs laugh or be looked at as wastes of space.

And so here I am, right in the middle of an academic shit show where the super smart dudes are sitting next to the seriously dumb dudes, surrounded by all the average dudes who live in fear of being called dumb. But everybody already knows where everybody else falls on the big brain curve—it's not exactly a secret.

We all remember who was blue and red and orange and purple in grades one through six, and who slid into levels one through five in grade seven. Nope, not a secret at all—and stuff like somebody's brainpower doesn't change over time either. Nobody morphs from orange to blue unless he knows how to cheat like a pro on spelling tests. And probably on math tests too.

"No worries, Sinclair," whispers Chad Walker, who spent most of grades one through six in orange with me until his mother called the principal and he somehow morphed into being red. "On the brain curve, your black X falls somewhere between the kids who memorized the dictionary over summer vacation"— he nods toward the front of the room, where brainiacs always sit—"and the kids who haven't quite figured out how to read." He turns around and looks at the kids who sit in a single row across the back, trying to look mean.

Sad fact is, I know for sure my black X falls *way* closer to the reading-challenged kids in the back. "So what does that make me, Walker?" I ask in a hushed voice because I'd definitely like to know. I don't expect an answer, though, and he doesn't give me one. All I know is, in elementary school, it made me orange. In seventh grade it made me level four in all academic classes. Now it just makes me pray I get a seat near the back of the classroom so I can hide.

And the worst part of Ms. Paloma's hetero-whatever grouping is Joey is in my class. While she passes out a paper that outlines World Geography's academic expectations, I let my brain wander back to the beginning of last year. Seventh grade was a big deal because we were too grown-up for elementary school, which made us officially not little kids anymore. And the very beginning of last September was when I figured out I had to quit playing kids' games with Joey if I wanted to survive in the middle-school wing. By the end of the first week of seventh grade, the Baker Street gang had dissolved like a cherry Lifesaver in a glass of Coke. Real quick,

Travis and me got the picture that we needed to be cool, and Emily and Lily got that they were girls and we weren't.

But Joey never figured out any of this stuff.

And when he came to my house in his mom's dress after the first day of grade seven, I knew better than to answer the door. If I got caught hanging out with "Josie," I was dead meat. For the rest of middle school, I'd be stuck sitting next to Joey on his front step, waiting for the school bus with my nose in a book and a target on my forehead, and I don't even like to read.

"Okay, class, please refer to the handout you have just received. Who can tell me what Roman numeral one says? Anybody?"

"Be punctual!" the brainiacs all call out, like they know something the rest of us don't. But no shit, Sherlock, because we can all read off a paper. I'm still thinking about foreheads, anyhow. Sometimes when I look at Joey, I remember the time he kissed me smack-dab on the middle of mine in his backyard. *And I liked it.*

That memory could get a guy killed, so for a few seconds, I make myself think about sounds whoopee cushions make when you plant your ass on them to clear my brain, in case there's a mind reader in World Geography. Farting sounds make kids laugh, but forehead kisses from other boys make kids dead.

It's not like I hate Joey—why should I? I just keep my distance. I don't have a death wish, so I don't have a choice.

I zone back in at the end of her lecture. "…. And that wraps up what I expect of my students this semester in grade eight World Geography class, which will provide for a smooth transition into Freshman World Cultures." When Ms. Paloma sends us her superior smile, I notice that there's a streak of brownish-red lipstick covering one of her front teeth. It makes her look like somebody slugged her in the mouth and a tooth got knocked out. I have to stick my hand over *my* mouth so she doesn't see me smirk because, for the most part, teachers frigging hate smirks. "The good news is that you needn't go it alone. I have taken the liberty of selecting study buddies for each of you. Your buddy will be your right hand."

A few guys giggle and mumble stuff like "but I'm a lefty," and the rest of us look around the room to predict our possible partners. Shit like who you work with in class matters in grade eight.

"Your study buddy is the one you will contact if you forget to write down the homework assignment in class, or if you want to review the spelling of states and capitals for a quiz. He or she will be there to help you with your projects and give you reassurance when you need it, because World Geography is a *very* challenging class."

I lay my head down sideways on the desk, waiting to find out who my right hand is going to be, and five minutes later, wouldn't you know it?

"Joseph Kinkaid, your study buddy is Eric Sinclair. Eric, please join Joseph at the desk beside his with your belongings."

"Damn it to hell and back," I mutter, but not loud enough for Ms. Paloma to hear. And for the record, I don't feel as guilty for swearing as I used to because Grandma's gone, and she was the only one who cared. And if there's ever been a good time to say "damn it to hell and back," it's right now. But I'm the kind of guy who follows the rules, so I toss my backpack over my shoulder and head to the front of the classroom where Joey's sitting with the other brainiacs and their new dumb partners.

"Hi, Eric," he says. I look away but can feel Joey gawking at my face. He's probably hoping to catch my eye and use his bewitching blue-eyed stare to hypnotize me into longing for the stellar best friendship we used to have.

And the sad fact is I haven't really talked to Joey since two summers ago. "Hey, Joe," I mumble. I call him Joe, even though in my head, he's still Joey. Joe sounds more grown-up. And less girly.

Princess! You used to call him Princess! my insides scream, but I tell them to shut the hell up.

"So I guess we're study buddies now," he says. I can hear the smile in his voice. My belly tightens into a ball and rolls over. This situation is risky.

"Looks like it." I'm fairly sure he's still watching me, but I decide it'd be better for both of us if I don't make eye contact with him at all. As in never during this entire semester. Because when I see those sparkling blue eyes, I feel guilty and rotten... and some other stuff. *Whatever.*

I tug on my earlobe to give me something to do. It still feels like the left side of my head got hit by a train in the general vicinity of my earlobe. On the bright side, the pain shakes me up and helps screw my brain back on straight.

"Maybe you could come over after school sometime, and we could study together and eat my mother's brownies like we used to," Joey suggests, probably looking all kinds of hopeful, but I have no proof of this, seeing as how I'm staring at a chewed-off pencil eraser on the floor between my feet.

What's so messed-up is that I sort of want to say, "Sure, dude, I'd be super pumped to come by some time. I missed hanging out with you so much I can't even put it into words, and I'd kill for one of your mom's ass-kicking brownies." If I did that, I'd probably end up with an A in geography. Plus Joey *was* a decent friend way back when, so maybe I'd even end up happy. But here at Wild Acres Middle School, dead meat, even *happy* dead meat with an A in geography, can't go to the boys' room without getting the living crap beat out of him.

Mrs. Kinkaid sure knew how to bake brownies good enough for the president to eat, though.

"Want a snack?" He asks me this every day after school.

And I pretty much always want a snack. Ever since spring, Mom says I been growing like a weed and eating her out of house and home, and since she boots me out the door to play pretty much the second I get home from school, there's no time to grab food. Not that we have much in our cabinets to grab, but Grandma makes sure we always got some apples and peanut butter and a loaf of bread. And sometimes Oreos.

Mom says Grandma's got a sweet tooth like me.

Joey goes outside right after school every day too. It's the only time his mom lets him wear a dress.

"Uh-huh," I say. "A snack'd be good."

These stupid memories aren't going to get me anywhere except maybe to a serious guiltfest because I dumped Joey quick, and then I pulled a cut and run like he had a catchy disease. I glance down at my desk and study the words kids before me carved into the wood, hoping for a distraction. Most of the words I see are ones Grandma didn't allow me to say, and probably wouldn't even want me to think. But she's living in Rhode Island at an old folks' home near Uncle Dave now, so I suppose she'll never find out. After I read them all, I take a deep breath and say, "I'm pretty sure I can't come over to study… seeing as I'm too busy playing soccer this fall." It's a lame excuse. I know it, and he knows it.

I don't wait around for Joey to start begging me, even if it'd feel good. I sit down at the desk beside him but pivot my chair in the opposite direction. "Heya, Travis!" I call across the aisle. "Lily's your study buddy? Good luck with *that*."

"Well, you got the Princess of Baker Street for your buddy! Maybe you can chase her down the hallway after class!"

This is going to be a very long year in World Geography.

3

AT THE end of geography class, Travis asked me over to his house for supper, and my head automatically nodded. What's messed-up is I *didn't* want to go just about as much as I *did* want to go. But almost nothing's more tempting to me than the thought of a home-cooked supper—since Grandma left, I've turned into the King of Frozen Pizza—so I said yes. There's one slight problem with going to the Jenkins' house, and there's no nice way to put it—Travis's dad scares the crap out of me.

My need for real food won out, so here I am.

"Call me Chuckie!" He hollers this in my face every time I step through their front door, and tonight is no exception. A good-sized glob of spit shoots forward from the wide gap between his two front teeth and lands on my nose, but I'm too nervous to wipe it off. So it dries there.

I feel like such a poser, calling Travis's dad by his first name like we're best pals, but the last time I was here, when I slipped up and called him Mr. Jenkins, he got a look in his eye that made me think he wanted to slug me. Hard.

Chuckie starts sucking down brews at the exact same time Travis and me start playing video games. And he doesn't sit in the kitchen with Mrs. Jenkins and have one of those "How was your day, dear?" chats married folks are supposed to have. Nope, the dude barges past Mrs. Jenkins, nearly knocking her over, to get to the living room. He's got a six-pack hooked on his super-strong pinkie finger—this kind of impresses me—and he drops his big butt on the couch in between Travis and me and starts ranting about the way we should play.

Chuckie calls it "coachin' us."

I call it screaming bloody murder.

Tonight he gets worked up much easier than last time I came over. "That was the stupidest move I ever seen a player make, Travis! Where'd you leave your brain—on the sidewalk in front of the house?"

"Dad, get a life! We're just playin' a stupid game!" When Travis shouts back, my belly crawls up inside my rib cage because I know things are going to go downhill fast.

"That's what you said last Saturday at the football game when you messed up on that block, remember? You said, 'Dad, it's just a game!'"

In two seconds Chuckie's chest is all puffed up and he's ready to body slam his very own kid. So I say in my most soothing voice, "Travis and Mr. Jenkins, you've got to calm down, or you're gonna break something for sure."

"Are you *stupid*, kid? Or have you got the world's shortest memory? I told you to call me Chuckie! *Chuckie!*"

"I… uh… I think…." I have no frigging clue what I think or don't think other than I think I'd like to disappear in a big puff of smoke, because all of a sudden *their* brawl is in the past tense, and Travis and Chuckie are looking for trouble in *my* direction.

"You *don't* think, and that's your problem, Eric. Right, Dad?"

"You said it, Travis. That there's a fact." Chuckie stands up, and I can't miss that he's ginormous. "Hey, Jessie! Where's our lousy dinner? You tryin' to starve us guys to death?"

"Hold your horses and come into the dining room—it's already on the table, Chuckie!" she hollers back.

When Chuckie heads to the bathroom to wash his hands, I follow Travis to the dining room. It smells so good in here— like a buttery, salty, meat and potato-filled heaven, and a kind of heaven I only get to visit when one of my friends invites me over to supper. But no joke, I'm still shaking from what *almost* went down with Travis's dad in the living room.

So here I sit at the dining room table, basically too scared to breathe, and at the same time, I'm sucking down Travis's mother's pot roast as fast as I can shovel it in. It's a trick—speed-eating without breathing—but I get it done. And the truth is, I'm dreaming about the moment when it's time to put my fork down and say, "Thanks, Mrs. Jenkins and Chuckie, but I've gotta get home because Mom's expecting me."

Even though she's not. She never has been. Never will be either.

WHEN I get home, I can't stop shaking, which sounds kind of lame, but a fact is a fact, even if it's a sad one. I'm so wigged out by Chuckie's anger-management issues—as Mr. Weeks, the middle school guidance counselor, calls it when Travis acts like an asshole—that I just can't calm down. For some reason it makes me feel better to curl into a tight ball on my bed and pull the sheets over my head. Another sad fact.

Life would be better if old houses didn't make so many creepy noises. There's a muffled scratching sound coming from somewhere over my head, and worse, the bedroom walls are creaking as if they're alive. It's like the cottage is talking to me, and it isn't saying, "Welcome home, Eric. I'm here to give you comfort and joy." Nope—it's more like the cottage's eyes are glowing red and it's growling, "Get oooooout!"

And the weirdest thing is, although I never actually seen my backyard neighbor's terrifying dog, Cujo, because he lives behind a tall wooden fence, I'm listening for the sound of his ferocious barking. Every now and then, when I think I hear it, I like it so much I smile a little. Cujo's barking lets me know I'm not the only living being left on earth. Or on Baker Street.

It's not like I plan what happens next. Tears don't exactly ask permission to drip down somebody's face. And they just start streaming down my cheeks like somebody turned a faucet on behind my stupid eyes. But nobody will ever know about how I'm wrapped up in my sheets, crying like a newborn baby who wants his bottle. Nobody can see me here in my bed, under my sheet. It's like I'm invisible.

Crying feels good—it gives me a shit-ton of relief. I decide to let myself bawl until it turns into tomorrow.

And so I do.

4

EVERY DAY at school, I'm starving by lunchtime, but especially today. All that's left in my cupboard at home are seventeen stale oyster crackers, a can of refried beans—and I can't find the can opener—and the moldy end slices of a loaf of bread that are falling out of an open plastic bag on the counter.

As soon as I sit down at the lunch table, I grab my hotdog and take a huge bite without bothering to douse it in the ketchup from the tiny paper cup on my tray. I swallow down a handful of tater tots before I even finish chewing. The burp that comes up from my belly is kind of legendary.

"That's disgusting, Sinclair," some asshole a few seats down the table wisecracks, but I tune whoever he is out and tear open my carton of chocolate milk. It takes about three gulps for me to suck the thing dry. I wish I had four more cartons.

In both of the elementary wings of the Wild Acres Grade School, we used to have to eat lunch with the other kids in our brain-level color group—I spent six years trading Fruit Roll-Ups with the same ten below-average students at the orange lunch table. Since last year we been allowed to sit wherever we want in the lunchroom, so like usual, I plant my butt with the other guys on the soccer team. The entire student body looks up to good athletes, and since I'm on the team, I'm allowed to sit here. I catch less crap at the jock table than I would anywhere else in the cafeteria.

Plus Mom always tells me, "You aren't exactly the sharpest tool in the shed, Eric, so stick with sports—they'll get you farther than your brain will." And so I do. I probably would have even if she didn't point this out to me on the nights we stand next to each other at the kitchen counter and scarf down our pizza, because nobody knows better than me that I'm as good at kicking balls as I'm lousy at doing word problems.

The thing is, tons of smack talk flies at lunch. Words go back and forth between the lunch tables, and most of them aren't what you'd call polite. I think of lunch tables as little planets at war. We all got our own planets we fight for—the jocks, the theater geeks, the brainiacs who share a table with the comic book traders, the artsy dudes, and the hot girls. But without the blue group *having* to sit with him, Joey's got nobody to plant *his* butt next to at lunch. And since the dude's got no home planet, he sits alone. Not safe and technically not my problem.

Every day's basically the same—it's like the lunchtime bullying plan is set in stone, and it's only the end of September. And it's way worse than it was last year, even though he sat alone then too. Travis gets to sit at the jock table, seeing as he's on the county football team. He starts in on Joey as soon as he sets his rear end on the bench and drops his lunch tray onto the sticky table. For Travis, "bullying Josie" is sort of like a bad habit he just can't kick. But I'm pretty sure he'd say it's more like a hobby he's real good at.

"All the way through sixth grade, Kinkaid wore a dress, like, *every day* after school—I kid you not." He announces this loud enough for the jocks and the entire hot-girl table, and of course, lonely Joey, to hear. And even though Joey wasn't hiding that he wore his mom's purple dress after school when we all played together, blabbing about it makes me feel like we're ratting him out.

An imaginary knife stabs into my gut and twists around. I try not to squirm and to keep my face blank, but it's next to impossible because my belly hurts like I'm having a baby.

"You've got to be kidding me—he wore a freaking dress?" Miles Maroney is always the first guy to jump in whenever things start getting mean and dirty. "But I betcha Josie looked cute, if you go for gays."

We all laugh, and I mean *all* of us.

I laugh even though I don't want to. Because I still remember how it was: Joey was the Princess of Baker Street, and Travis and Emily and Lily and me all looked up to him as much as middle school kids look up to the guys on the soccer team now. Joey was the neighborhood kid with all the best ideas. None of us cared what he wore out to play—not even Travis.

"What a freaking princess!" yells Noah Mayer, and we all laugh some more because Noah is the starting forward on the soccer team, and we pretty much *have to* laugh at everything he says when he's trying to be funny, or he won't pass to us. Maybe I forgot to pay my brain bill, but I know how shit like this works.

Joey's eyes stay glued to his book. For a second I wonder what he's reading because, back when we were kids, his mom read him the best books at bedtime, and he told us all about them. Then he actually took us there. The gang from Baker Street followed Joey into a giant peach and to a chocolate factory and onto a pirate ship in the sky. It was awesome.... I've never been back to those places since.

"What's the matter, Princess Josie? Frog Prince got your tongue?"

"Well, nobody else is gonna french kiss Joey Kinkaid, that's for sure!"

I don't pay much attention to who says what. Through my shaggy bangs, my gaze is stuck on Joey, who says nothing at all. As usual he doesn't stick up for himself; he just closes his eyes like he's wishing it would all go away. And I close my eyes too because I wouldn't mind if this whole nasty scene disappeared into a big puff of smoke. With my eyes closed and my mind on Joey, I start remembering things I wish I could forget, like how his hair smelled—as sweet as the soft kind of sugary pink bubble gum.

And smells stick with you....

The princess leans over, and her long hair falls all over my face. "Your hair mostly smells like No More Tears Baby Shampoo,

21

and a little bit like Bubble Yum too," I tell her. I don't brush the feathery-light strands off my face, not even off my mouth, 'cause I like how it feels in a weird way.

Princess Ariel says, "Mermaids don't need to shampoo their hair. The ocean keeps it clean."

This makes lots of sense.

There's plenty about Joey I can't forget, and I'm honestly not sure if I really want to. The stuff I did with the Baker Street gang fills up all of the bright parts of my memory bank. The rest of the stuff I remember about being a kid, except for times with Grandma, are mostly dark and gray.

"Gotta hit the boys' room," I say, and I mean it. Nobody's listening, though. They're too focused on their favorite hobby—torturing Princess Josie—whose head is bowed over his book as I pass by him. I don't think he's reading, though, because his cheeks are about as red as the ketchup on his hotdog. Plus his eyes are still closed.

I end up racing down the hall to the boys' room. I can't get there quick enough unless I want to crap my pants in public. And I sure don't want to do that because the guys would start calling me Eric Sin-crap or something like that.

The worse thing is that seeing Joey all bent out of shape reminds me of the sad truth: I'm more scared of standing alone than I am of standing on the right side. Which is beside Joey.

Guilt sucks.

When the knife in my gut twists, I know it won't be safe for me to leave the bathroom anytime soon. Looks like Mr. Carr is going to have to send out a search party to look for me when I don't show up for math class. I hope he doesn't send Travis, Miles, or Noah to find me. I'll never hear the end of it.

5

I MUST be depressed because I'm lying on my bed, wrapped in my stinky sheets, and it's not even bedtime. I spent a while trying to puff my pillow up enough so my back didn't hurt when I leaned on it to do my homework, but it didn't work. My pillow is way too much like a pancake to make a decent backrest. So I gave up on homework, and now I'm just lying flat, looking up at the ceiling stains.

Being alone most of the time bites, so sometimes I close my bedroom door and pretend Mom and Grandma are in the living room watching *The Bachelor* on TV like they used to. In my bedroom, living a fantasy that the two people who love me are at the end of the hallway, is much more relaxing than hanging out over at Travis's house. When I came home from dinner at the Jenkins' house last week, my belly was nice and full, but I shook for the rest of the night because I was so freaked out by the look in Chuckie's eyes when I accidentally called him Mr. Jenkins.

So instead of wondering where Mom might be right now, or whether Chuckie is going to sneak into my bedroom and take revenge on me in my sleep, I think about Joey. It's weird, but as I spend more time sitting beside him in class, memories of us as little kids don't pop up in my brain quite so much. Probably it's because I can obsess over what us two have going on in the here and now. I don't think I'm ever going to wish those old memories away, though, because maybe I *like* them. Maybe memories of playing with Joey are some of the best things I got to think about. Besides, nobody has a right to know about my private Joey thoughts except me.

I'm going to take a quick nap and then figure out what to do about my sorry World Geography notebook.

As a study buddy, Joey's the best. He's already saved my ass at least five times in World Geography class, and it's only been two weeks since we got partnered together. I expect this number will go up. Up as in over the moon, because I'm not too good at stuff like labeling topography. And Joey is.

To be safe we only talk to each other through email outside of class.

It mostly goes like this: I send him a question that proves exactly how clueless I am when it comes to world geography, and Joey writes back to me within three minutes, like he's sitting there at his kitchen table, twiddling his thumbs and waiting for me to email him. One time he email-explained the directions to a project where we had to map the climate regions of the world because I didn't get it when Ms. P told us in class. Another time he email-outlined all of my ideas so I could write a paragraph that made sense comparing the Mississippi River to the Amazon.

Joey seriously should be a teacher. Even in emails, he's good at explaining stuff. But still, I can't be seen with him at school or in the town library… or anywhere. It would be like social death for me, if "social death" translates into me getting smacked down in the locker room every day at the end of soccer practice for being Princess Josie's boyfriend.

I think Joey gets this. He isn't stupid. But still, what it comes down to is I'm a crappy friend. And tonight I should really slice-and-bake him some chocolate chip cookies because I got a big favor to ask. Not that I have a tube of cookie dough, but I wish like hell I did. I'd eat a quarter of it raw and *then* bake cookies for Joey.

I sit cross-legged on my bed, prop my computer on my lap, and open my emails.

Sinclair7@lifecast.net
Hey, Joe.
*This is gonna surprise you (not) but my notes
suck and I don't think they're gonna get me a
passing grade on the notebook check tomorrow in
World Geo. Can I borrow your notebook tonight
and copy your notes?*
Eric

Kinkaidfam@lifecast.net
*Sure. Want me to ask Mom if she'll drive me
over to your house with my notebook? We're all
cleaned up from dinner, so I'm sure she won't mind.*
Joey

Sinclair7@lifecast.net
*No, that's OK. It'll only take me ten minutes
to walk to your place. Is it OK if I come over?*

Kinkaidfam@lifecast.net
It's great. I'll be waiting for you.

I kill time for ten minutes so I don't get to Joey's house creepily quickly. I can't have the school's biggest social outcast thinking *I'm* a needy loser. That would be hitting an all-time low.

Mom and me live in a cottage she inherited when Grandma moved into some old folks' home for "active seniors" four hours away in Rhode Island, near Uncle Dave's fancy house. I love Grandma's place, but I liked it better when Grandma lived here too. As I circle around the cottage, I can't miss the peeling red paint on the house, the overgrown grass, and the front door that seems to be perched in midair, three feet above the ground.

25

Nobody takes care of a thing around here, so when the front steps fell off the house last winter, they never got put back on. Now we come and go through the kitchen door out back.

I run all the way down Baker Street, and when I'm finally standing on the sidewalk, looking up the walkway at the Kinkaids' big lemon mansion, it hits me how weird it is that two houses so completely different can be on the same street. My house looks rickety, like a gentle Temperate Marine ocean breeze—I learned about this climate region in World Geography—could knock it over. Or at least blow the back porch off, which would probably be a good thing because it's seriously hazardous. But Joey's house looks sturdy enough for the president to live in.

Joey's house is bright yellow and brand-new looking, even though it's been here as long as I can remember. The grass is as green as a four-leaf clover and is always mowed perfect, like the Wild Acres Country Club's golf course. The shrubs are trimmed to look like a row of mini-Christmas trees, and the walkway hasn't got *one* lonely weed growing up between the bricks. Even the mailbox is spotless and shiny and has a painting on it of *another* cheery yellow house with golf course grass and tiny Christmas trees in front. The best thing is that Mrs. Kinkaid's kind face is usually in the window.

It's like the sun is always shining at Joey's house.

I grow a ginormous lump in my throat as I stand here gawking at the prettiest house on the street because I live with a crapload of guilt over dumping the kid who lives in it the heartless way I did. Joey never did anything to me except be my best friend from grade one until the first day of grade seven when he showed up at my house in his mother's dress. And what makes it a million times worse is that I'd dump him all over again if it meant saving my butt from getting stuck out on a window ledge, cold and alone.

I swallow the lump down, but the stupid thing pops right back up.

Guilt sucks.

It's a mental challenge to make myself walk up this walkway—I get sweaty and then goose pimpled and then sweaty again, all in twenty steps. But still I go for it. I need a decent grade on my notebook, and sucking knowledge out of Joey's brain is the only way I'm going to get it.

Before I even knock, Mrs. Kinkaid throws open the door, just like she does every morning when she watches Joey climb onto the school bus. Right now she's got this humongous grin on her face, where on school mornings she looks like she's watching the "stab the girl next door" part of a horror movie. "Eric, it's been so long since you've come over to play with Joey," she says like she's the happiest mother on earth. *And* she smells good.

But—*I'm thirteen years old, lady. Don't you know I'm too old to play?*

"Hey, Mrs. Kinkaid."

"I baked brownies for you boys."

"Uh… thanks." Again I try to swallow back that huge lump, but it stays put, sending me a message that it isn't planning to go anywhere anytime soon, so I better figure out how to deal with it. "Is Joey around?" I ask in a raspy, lumpy-throated voice.

"Of course. He's at the kitchen table waiting for you. And the brownies… they're still warm."

"Great, and like I said, thanks." I fight the urge to thank her over and over again, because I could get stuck in "thank you oh so very much, ma'am" mode real easy and come off looking lame. It's just rare anybody does special stuff, like bake brownies, for me… or wait for me at their kitchen table. Still I shrug like I couldn't care less about homemade brownies or my World Geography notebook or my secret friend, Joey, and then I head to the kitchen. I already know where it is since I been here plenty of times when I was a kid.

Joey's sitting at the table with his hands folded on top of his notebook. He looks different at school, and I think it's because he's not dressed in his usual goofy tan pants, ironed so they're as stiff as a paper plate, with a razor-sharp line down the front of each leg that you could cut cheese with, and one of those fancy button-collared shirts. Tonight he's wearing a soft yellow T-shirt with a picture of a fuzzy gray kitten on the front and the kind of pants my mom used to wear when she was doing yoga on the living room floor. His hair isn't pulled back off his face like it always is at school. It's falling over his shoulders—smooth and silky, like it just got brushed. I'm not too sure why I care about Joey's long blond hair, but I do.

And the kitchen smells like warm chocolate. All of a sudden, my eyes get wet, and I don't know why, but I blink and blink until they're dry again.

"Hello, Eric. Come sit down." He seems to somehow know I'm in the room, because he doesn't look up at me. I fake a yawn and sniff my armpits real casual, but I don't smell anything that would alert him to me being here. Then I go over to the table, drop my notebook on it, and pull out a chair. I stand still for a few seconds before I plant my butt.

Swallowing my worries about getting caught coming here by the other kids at school was a big step for me. And it's not like anybody gets on my case if my grades suck—Mom never even asks to look at my dumb report cards, so I got pretty good over the past couple years at faking her signature. I even make a tiny heart over the I in Sinclair, the way she does. But for some reason, *I* want to see decent marks in the little boxes. Maybe it's my only way of getting a pat on my back from a grown-up, but probably I just like to see concrete proof that I'm not an idiot.

Joey opens his notebook. Inside the pale-blue lines on the paper are scrawled rows upon rows of words—all printed in tiny, perfect letters—surrounded by drawings of a castle and a unicorn and a waterfall. He drew the pictures with a regular number-two pencil, but I see a rainbow of colors because, even after all this time, I know how Joey's imagination works. The castle is made of pale-gray stone and has a purple flag flying from the center of the turret on the side. The unicorn is fuzzy and pink, with a sparkly golden horn. And the waterfall sprays down buckets of aqua-blue water that remind me of the ocean in the vacation postcards Lily sent to Travis and me when she went to the Bahamas last year on February vacation.

I want to tell him the drawings are awesome, but I sit there with my finger up my nose. Well, it's not *really* up my nose, but it's what Mom says I look like when I can't come up with the right words, and I clam up.

"Go ahead and have a brownie. Mom made them especially because you were coming over."

I shrug again and grab one—can't exactly stop myself since they smell like the next best thing to meat-and-potatoes heaven. And when I shove a warm fudgy corner into my mouth, it's like taking a bite of the past. Memories of Joey and me being best friends surge until I swallow the brownie down, along with the lump in my throat.

"We should start by comparing what you've written down and what I've written down. Did you date your notes?" he asks.

"For the most part I did, I think," I reply. We both flip to what we took for notes on the first few days of school. And then together we look at what I scribbled down.

"Now look at my notes. What do I have that you don't have?"

I check out the first few pages of Joey's notebook. "All the stuff about the mountain ranges in North America."

"Right." He picks up an index card from a pile on the table and a black ballpoint pen, and then slides them toward me. "Copy everything I wrote about mountain ranges on this. Then we can staple it into your notebook."

"'Kay."

Joey smiles, and I get to work. He proceeds to help me pick out what's missing from each page and copy it all onto index cards.

Within an hour I got everything stapled in my notebook that Joey's got in his. It's kind of like a miracle occurred in his kitchen.

And it's still light outside when we finish. Part of me wants to grab my *now*-brainiac notebook, jump to my feet, and run out the door since I got what I wanted here. But I'm not that much of a jerk.

I owe him one, right?

Or maybe it's time to be real: Joey's a pretty cool guy, and I'm not ready to leave him yet. I don't want to think too hard about the reason I ask him, "Wanna go for a walk before I head home?"

"Sure." The way he rises up from the chair and floats to the door is so graceful. Furry boots he doesn't wear to school are waiting on the doormat, and he carefully slides his feet in. "Mom, I'm going outside to take a walk with Eric!"

"Just for ten minutes, Joey—it's going to be dark soon," she calls back from upstairs. Their little exchange reminds me of when I was too young for school and Grandma kept track of me.

"Let's go out the back door and walk down the path to the pump house," I suggest.

Nobody can see us together, or I'm dead meat. This much I know.

For a split second, Joey and me catch eyes. He knows exactly why I don't want to walk down the sidewalk along Baker Street with him. He gets that I'm ashamed to be seen with him, but still he nods.

Sweat drips down my face, and my armpits prickle.

Guilt sucks.

And just like he knows I'm hiding him, *I* know that I'm going to keep on letting Joey live out my biggest fear at school: being stuck on a high and dangerous window ledge—scared and alone—with hundreds of curious eyeballs glued to him, waiting to see if he falls or jumps or lives to see another day.

I follow Joey out the back door of the kitchen onto his deck, and when the breeze blows through my too-long brown curls, it feels good on my neck. I'm sweating buckets, and not pretty pails of aqua-blue water like in Joey's waterfall drawing, but stinky buckets of guilty sweat. I can't think of anything to say as we step off the deck, head across his backyard, cut through a row of trees, and trot onto the path.

For a long time, we walk in total silence. To end the awkward moment, I point to some marks on a hemlock tree. "See this? These are teeth marks. Deer chew on this kind of tree in the winter when the snow is deep, even though it's not their favorite. That way they save energy, rather than walking all around the forest looking for other kinds of plants."

"I didn't know that," Joey says. He stops and runs his fingers over the marks on the tree.

I feel smarter than I ever did in my whole entire life. It's an amazing feeling—kind of like I just sucked down a Red Bull in a single gulp. We keep walking, and when I see a dead tree that's still standing, I tell Joey, "Dead trees are shelter for wildlife." He looks at me with such fascination that I add, "The hollowness makes awesome nesting places for flying squirrels."

"I didn't know that either." Joey's wispy blond eyebrows shoot up an entire inch. He is actually spellbound by *me*. I want to be cool, so I don't grin, but it's one of the hardest things I've had to do in eons. And Joey's as good a listener as he is a teacher. I'm so glad I paid attention when I went on those sweltering and endless nature hikes in summer camp last July.

"The bugs in there feed animals and birds." I'm guessing on this one, but Joey smiles like he used to do when he was a princess and I was a knight and I said the right thing.

"You know a lot about nature, Eric."

"I know the difference between softwoods and hardwoods too." I'm bragging now.

"Where did you learn all of this information?"

"I went to cam—" I change my mind about filling him in on the Wild Acres Kids Meet Mother Nature Summer Camp I got into for free because Mom and me are *financially challenged.* "I just know it, I guess." A guy doesn't have to give up all his secrets.

Pretty soon it's not even a tiny bit awkward to be alone and walking so close together. Joey dares to bring up real-life topics. "How do you like being on the soccer team?" he asks.

"It's okay, I guess. I'm not a starter, but I get decent playing time."

"Maybe you'll be a starter next year." *Nobody* ever encourages me. I take a quick peek at his face to make sure he's for real.

When I decide Joey's being legit, I respond with a little truth of my own. "I hope I start on the high school JV team next year, but I'm not exactly Coach Petrassi's favorite, so I don't get enough playing time to improve too much." I can't believe it, but I'm actually going to tell him the rest. "Almost every day he announces to the whole team that my practice jersey stinks to high heaven and says he doesn't blame them if they won't come anywhere near me." We're almost to the pump house at the end of the path. "Do you play any sports?" He's not on the school teams, but maybe he's a professional ice skater or something, and I just don't know about it because he does it on his own, seeing as Wild Acres Elementary School doesn't have an ice skating rink.

Joey shakes his head. "No sports. All I do is take an adult ballroom dance class at the community house on Saturday mornings."

"That's cool, but why do you take a dance class for grown-ups? You could go to Miss Jeannie's School of Dance downtown. That's where Emily goes. She says that she loves tap dance the best because she's got a lot of rhythm."

Joey's quiet for a few seconds. He squints as he studies the pond in front of us. Finally he answers. "I fit in better with grown-ups."

I wrinkle my nose because I don't get it—most grown-ups make me feel guilty, kind of like I stole something. "Maybe we should go back to your house. It's getting dark, and your mom wants you home." It hits me as soon as we turn around—of course he fits in better at dance class with grown-ups—the girls who dance at Miss Jeannie's tease him as much as the boys do. Except for Emily. She's not mean, just a little bossy.

It's so quiet on the walk back to his house that I can hear the traffic passing by, right through the woods on Baker Street. I'm not sure what he's obsessing over, but *I'm* busy worrying about how Joey's going to survive the rest of middle school as the number-one social outcast. I steal a glance at him. And I wish I didn't think it, but I do: *he's so pretty.*

Joey's always been pretty to me.

I remember this day a long time ago that we made the world's best fairy house in the woods right near where we're walking right now….

"It's perfect," Princess says. She's right. This is the best fairy house we made since we turned seven. "Rise to your feet, my brave knight."

We both stand up and look at each other.

"You and I will live in this tiny castle together, and you will be my prince."

My face gets hot, but I nod because the idea sounds real good. She's the prettiest girl I know, and when Princess leans forward and kisses my forehead, I don't tell her that kisses are only for family.

It all changes when Princess shouts, "Chase me!" and runs across the grass.

"I'll follow you everywhere!" I yell, and I mean it.

I decide to go home before I say something stupid, and probably also true.

When we're in sight of his house, I race toward the street and yell, "See yah tomorrow!"

I forget that I left my brainiac notebook at Joey's house until I get home, and by then it's too late to go back because Joey's probably already tucked into his bed. But I know my study buddy has got my back, and he'll bring it to school tomorrow for the World Geography notebook check.

6

TRAVIS, LILY, and me are walking home from school today at four o'clock because we all got detentions again. My detention was on account of more missing math homework—Mr. Carr is not what you'd call happy with me these days. There's nothing new about this. Travis and Lily got detention for bullying Joey on the school bus this morning, which isn't big news either. It happens on more days than it doesn't.

"Why don't you guys lay off the kid?" I'm mad because Joey never did anything to them except be nice, and they insist on torturing him.

"He's just *so annoying*, you know?" Lily rolls her eyes. "And here's the question you *should* be asking, Eric—why does Joey Kinkaid always wear those ridiculous tan pants and those nerdy checkered button-up shirts? He looks like somebody's grandpa going to the golf course, not a kid going to middle school."

I can answer this question without sounding like I'm defending Joey. "You remember Mrs. Kinkaid from when we were kids—she's like an old-fashioned mom," I explain. "The lady probably buys Joey's clothes at one of the fancy department stores at the mall and gets him the stuff she thinks is proper and respectable." I tug up my loose-fitting jeans that are even baggier than usual because I've worn them ten times without washing them and they're all stretched out. Mom hasn't done laundry in forever. Plus I lost track of my belt.

In fact, I haven't seen Mom hardly at all this week. I think she comes by the cottage during the day when I'm at school. A couple of times last week when I skipped soccer practice and came home early, Mom was there doing laundry—but just her own stuff, not mine. I felt as if I was catching her being sneaky—like she was hoping I wouldn't notice she was there. The thing is, most kids notice their long-lost mothers.

Anyhow, I pretty much always wear plain white T-shirts. Mom says they're the cheapest kind of shirt at Walmart, and I catch zero crap for wearing them until they start turning bluish-gray from being washed with my jeans. Lucky for me, the only thing that really matters, as far as what boys wear goes, is that I got cool high-tops. And Grandma usually gets me a decent pair of Nikes for Christmas every year, so I'm covered. This year I got them in a box that came in the mail because she spent Christmas in Rhode Island.

"I don't know why, really, but just looking at Joey makes me want to slap him," Lily confesses. "So I *did*. You know, I slapped him. It's not a crime."

"It kind of is," I mumble, but she's not listening.

"I swear he thinks he's a girl. And that's just wrong," she adds like she's trying to prove something to me.

Travis smiles, and his bushy brows knit together into a single long, hairy line. Wearing this creepy unibrow grin, he sends Lily two thumbs-up and declares, "Joey Kinkaid deserves everything he gets and then some—he needs to be taught a lesson." Maybe it's Travis's voice I hear, but it sure sounds like Chuckie's words, which reminds me of how Mom used to say the apple doesn't fall too far from the tree.

It makes sense with Travis and Chuckie, but Mom is *my* tree, and if I'm her apple, it means I'm never going to graduate from high school. Still, I take a few steps away from Travis and Lily, not caring that it means I'm practically walking in the middle of Baker Street. I'm pissed off to the max, and I can't hide it. What they do to Joey is so rotten it makes me not want to be anywhere near them, even if it means getting arrested for jaywalking.

This morning on the bus, Lily sat beside Joey, and Travis sat behind him, and they basically took turns slapping his cheeks and the back of his head for the entire ride to school. I'm not sure who ratted them out, but Vice Principal Eickler kept Travis and Lily after school today to tell them she saw what they did on the school bus video. In no uncertain terms, she let them know if they bully Joey on the bus again, they'll lose their bus-riding privileges until winter vacation.

Even though they're my best friends, part of me wishes Vice Principal Eickler didn't give them a second chance. I hated seeing Joey as upset as he was when he got to school today. His face was all red—partly from getting slapped, but mostly from being embarrassed—and his long hair was all messed up, not smooth and silky like usual. And maybe he wasn't crying, but *I* nearly was. I was just so pissed off at Travis and Lily, but mostly I was pissed off at myself because I just sat there, two seats behind, watching them torture him. I had to spend first period in the nurse's office because my belly wouldn't quit aching until I calmed down.

"I'm not gonna mess with him on the bus anymore, 'cause I can't get up early enough to walk to school every day," Travis explains. "But I got a new plan. I'm not gonna let him take a piss in the boys' bathroom by our lockers anymore. He doesn't belong in there 'cause he's a total girl."

"Joey Kinkaid can't pee in the girls' room, Travis. That would be so wrong," Lily argues like she's mad, but she's smiling.

"Maybe Vice Principal Spike-ler will have to set up a 'safe place' for the kid to take a piss, like at the nurse's office," Travis tells us with another one of those evil unibrow grins.

"Get a life," I mutter, again under my breath. But instead of arguing anymore, I change the subject because it's easier and way less risky than trying to get my point across. "You guys catch the Red Sox game last night?"

7

I'M OVER at Joey's house again. Tonight Mrs. Kinkaid invited me to eat dinner before we started studying for our World Geography test. Mom doesn't care that I'm not going to be home for dinner tonight, which is mostly always frozen pizza we eat while leaning on the kitchen counter. I know for a fact she won't care because she isn't going to be home either, on account of her having a new boyfriend. Some dude named Robby.

I've only seen her at dinnertime twice in the past five days, not that I'm counting, and they're what I call "drive-by dinners." She microwaves the pizzas, pops open a couple of Cokes if we got them, and asks me what's up, but she starts playing on her phone before I have a chance to answer. On the bright side, she's been in a good mood lately, and she'll stay in a good mood until Robby cheats on her. Or starts drinking too much booze. Or moves into our cottage without paying rent while cheating on her *and* drinking until he can't walk a straight line. This is usually the direction her relationships take.

Tonight Joey's dad is home too. He travels a lot for his important business job, so there are two versions of the Kinkaid family. When Mr. Kinkaid is away, everything's chill. Joey and his mom eat dinner whenever they're hungry, sometimes in front of the widescreen TV in the living room—a big deal for them, but not so much for me. Well, the widescreen TV is a big deal for me, but not the watching TV at dinnertime part because it's what I do whenever Mom's not home. When I'm over at their house and it's just the three of us, they talk about fun stuff like how Mrs. Kinkaid found a new stained-glass window coloring book for Joey's massive coloring book collection, or they do goofy things like taking turns trading their favorite Disney movie lines. I kind of wish it could be like this at my house. But then I'd need a different mom.

Everybody acts real stiff with Mr. Kinkaid sitting at the dinner table, though. Maybe it's not as scary for me as going to eat supper with Travis and Chuckie, but it's still pretty awkward.

"So, Eric, I've missed seeing you around here for, what, the past year or so?" Mr. Kinkaid's first job is to remind me I dumped his kid the split second we hit the middle-school wing of Wild Acres Grade School.

I stare guiltily at Mr. Kinkaid, and my mouth drops open because I can't come up with a smart reply. But I shut my trap quick when I remember how Mom says I'll catch flies this way. And Joey's dad, who is still expecting an answer, makes me think of a burly football player in a snug button-up business shirt and a loosened tie instead of skintight pants and a numbered jersey with shoulder pads underneath. He's blond, with a square head and a body that's shaped like a *V*, stern blue eyes, and a smirk, even when he's chewing. I half expect him to yell, "Green nineteen, green nineteen, forty-three, set—pass the rolls and butter—hut!"

But he just says, "Well?"

I look at Joey for some help, but he's staring into his bowl of beef stew.

Mrs. Kinkaid ends up saving my ass. "Actually, Kevin, Eric has been studying with Joey quite a lot since they became study buddies in eighth grade World Geography class. Right, boys?"

"Yes, ma'am," I reply, and Joey nods.

"Joey tells me you're on the soccer team." It sounds like he's accusing me of a crime.

"That's right, sir."

"Does your team have a winning record?"

"So far we do. We won three games and lost only one." I'm nervous answering his questions, like I'm taking a test I'm not ready for.

"Over the summer I told Joe that he should try out for soccer or football, or even cross-country. But he takes *dance class*." Mr. Kinkaid shakes his head sharply, but his short blond hair stays exactly in its proper place like it's painted on. It's kind of like a magic trick, but I try not to gawk because Mom used to say staring was rude, back in the old days when she had a clue I was alive.

And I don't like the way Mr. Kinkaid's face is twisted and angry right now. It's suddenly way too quiet around the fancy dining room table, and I get the same shaky feeling as I do when I eat dinner with Travis and Chuckie. And for no good reason, I think of roadkill....

I lose sight of Princess for a second when she goes around her house into the side yard. And when I come around, I see she's not running anymore. She's standing real still, looking across the yard at a big vulture on the edge of Baker Street. And she's crying.

Before I start running toward her to ask what's wrong, Princess turns and puts one finger against her lips to shush me. I stare at her. I swear that buckets of tears are pouring down her cheeks, and her face is all wrinkled up, just like my nose gets when I'm confused. She looks as pretty when she's crying as she does when she's smiling—it's just a sad kind of pretty, like a girl on a "Please forgive me" greeting card.

Instead of running to her side, I tiptoe. "That's a turkey vulture eating roadkill," I whisper and feel sort of smart. We watch for a minute as the big bird rips at the furry skin of the dead animal. "I think it's eating a squirrel, maybe."

"No, it's not." I can tell regular Joey is back because his voice sounds like a kid's, not a grown-up lady's. "That's my dad and me."

"Are you the roadkill or the vulture?" I ask.

"I'm the one who's getting ripped into pieces." And his voice sounds different than regular Joey or Princess. He sounds mad, I think.

"Then you're the roadkill." A whole bunch of questions about why Joey's dad is a vulture pops into my head, but before I can ask, he's talking again.

"Dad wants me to be a prince instead of a princess when we play." He pats down the skirt part of his mom's sundress so it lies flat against his legs.

That doesn't make any sense at all, so I wrinkle my nose some more. "But you're the Princess of Baker Street."

Joey doesn't smile at me like he usually does when I say something good. He wipes his eyes with his wrist and gawks at the vulture. "Chase me," he says, but he doesn't start running. He just keeps on staring.

This memory solves the mystery of why I'm sitting here at the Kinkaids' fancy dinner table, thinking about run-over rodents.

"Kevin, dear, Joey *enjoys* ballroom dance," Mrs. Kinkaid says in a trembling voice. She sounds as shaky as I feel.

"For God's sake, Greta, ballroom dance class is for elderly women with knee replacements who need to elevate their heart rates, not for healthy young boys." The way Mr. Kinkaid rips off a chunk of his roll, dips it into his bowl, and rubs it all around in the gravy makes me feel sick. "Why don't you pick a sport and play it, Joe? Like Eric does." He pops the bread into his mouth and waits for a reply before chewing.

He gets no answer. Joey's face is all red, the same way it gets in the cafeteria when the jocks are torturing him. Mrs. Kinkaid's cheeks are bright red too. And *I* think, by now, Mr. Kinkaid ought to know Joey's into stuff like drawing pictures and dancing and being the smartest kid in the middle school, not playing soccer and football. Maybe he knows this stuff, but he just doesn't care.

I'm not good at facing off with people, though, so I change the subject. I'm *really* good at this. "Mrs. Kinkaid, your beef stew is awesome. Best I ever had." It's not a lie.

41

"Thank you, Eric." Mrs. Kinkaid looks at me for a second and then at her husband. I'm not sure why, but I feel bad for her. She licks her lips because she's nervous and brushes back her short brown curls, then tries to sell Joey's worthiness to his father. "Joey helped me make dinner, you know, Kevin. He's quite a good little cook."

Joey glances up from his bowl, probably hoping for a "way to go, son," but all he gets from his dad is a scowl. Then Mr. Kinkaid shakes his head one more time and mumbles, "It figures."

"Please excuse me," Joey squeaks and then hops out of his chair and bolts for the stairs.

It's hard for me to swallow my last bite of stew because that annoying lump pops up in my throat again. When I finally force the bite of stew down, I clear my throat and say, "Dinner sure was good… and, you know, can I be excused too?"

When Mr. Kinkaid replies, "Be my guest," I don't wait around for an extra second. I race for the stairs about as fast as Joey did.

Once I get to his room, I knock on the door, even though it's standing wide open. "Can I come in?"

Joey looks like he got splattered, belly-down, on the bed. His arms and legs are sticking out, and his face is stuffed into the pillow.

But he doesn't say no, so I go in and stand beside the bed. "You okay, Joe?"

He shakes his head back and forth.

"You mad at your dad?"

His head moves back and forth again.

"If you're not mad, then why are you lying flat on your belly like a pancake getting fried in a pan?"

When I see Joey's shoulders shake, I know he's laughing, and I'm surprised at how glad I am.

"You aren't a pancake, dude, so something's gotta be wrong."

42

Joey rolls over onto his back and looks up at me. Some of his blond hair is stuck to his face with tears. "I'm not exactly the son my dad would have picked."

"You're a great son, Joe."

"Maybe Mom thinks so, but Dad knows that I'm not...." He doesn't finish his thought, and I don't try to make him.

"Let's go out in your backyard and kick a soccer ball around for a while. I can show you how it's done," I offer.

"I don't have a soccer ball," Joey says.

"Well, have you got any ball at all?"

"I think there's a red rubber ball in the garage."

"That'll work." I reach out my hand, and Joey takes it. I pull him off the bed. "Come on."

When he gets to his feet, he asks, "What about studying?"

"We can study after soccer lessons. It's not that important."

"Are you sure?"

"Course I am." I watch as he grabs an elastic band from off his bureau and pulls his long hair up into a ponytail on the top of his head. "Let's go."

Five minutes later we're kicking the ball around his backyard. Mr. Kinkaid watches us out the big window in the kitchen. He's not smiling or frowning—he's just watching with straight-line lips. And the truth is, if Joey had wanted to try out for the soccer team, I think he would have made it. He's got good aim and a powerful kick—the dude's "a natural," which is what Coach Petrassi always says about Noah Mayer.

8

"LILY TOLD me you're doing way better than her in geography class. She said Ms. Paloma even announced that you had one of the top-five highest grades in the class on your last test." Emily looks at me skeptically, like she thinks I used cheat notes. Her high ponytail swings back and forth as she shakes her head, and then she gives me a serious mommy look. "Not to be rude, but what's up with that?"

Emily doesn't have what Mom calls "a mean streak" in her. She can be bossy and maybe a little bit whiny, but she's never nasty. Right now she's just wondering what's up with my stellar geography grades, not trying to let me know she thinks I'm too dumb to get a B+. So I level with her. "I been getting a little help."

"From a friend in the class?"

I shrug. I'm not so much hiding my relationship with Joey from Emily as I'm not really clear on how to answer her question. I'm not sure I can call him a friend, and I'm about positive he can't call me one.

"So who's helping you?" she asks.

"Just a kid," I reply.

Emily and I are always sit-up partners in gym class. At the moment she's got a tight grip on my ankles, and I'm doing what I do best: physical stuff. Cranking out fifty sit-ups is too easy, so when I hit seventy-five, I brush my hair off my sweaty face. My stupid bangs are too thick to see through now—don't think I ever went this long before without a haircut. But what's a guy supposed to do when his mom hasn't been around on the weekends to take him to Supercuts? At least Mom's boyfriend, Robby, isn't living with us.

44

"Does 'just a kid' have a name?" Emily asks.

"Yeah… Joey's my study buddy, and he's saving my grade."

"*Our* Joey from Baker Street?" I watch Emily's face for signs of *ewwww*, but I don't see any. "I swear, he's the smartest kid in our entire grade. I'm in English class with him, and *he* teaches Mr. Lyons stuff about the books we're reading."

I nod, not at all surprised. "Your turn. Lie down on the mat."

Emily and I switch places. After she does a couple of sit-ups, she asks, "Remember how we used to chase him up and down Baker Street?"

"Joey?"

She nods and does a few more sit-ups. "We called him our princess."

He *was* our princess… our leader.

Even though it's not a funny moment, next thing I know, I'm smiling. I remember how when we were kids, we used to chase Joey at lunch recess too. But one day in second grade, Mrs. Robinson, the recess monitor, told Joey we couldn't play princess at school anymore. She said we had to be birds instead, probably because she thought it was wrong Joey liked to pretend he was a girl. So Joey decided to be a *Swan* Princess. I even laugh a little because he outsmarted a grown-up who was sticking her nose into our kid business, where it didn't belong.

"What's so funny?" Emily asks when she's flat on her back.

I'm not about to tell her I was thinking of how we used to pretend we were birds at lunch recess in second grade. So I say, "Remember the color groups we were all divided into in the elementary school wings? Joey was in blue, the brainiac color."

I say this like it's no big deal, but I wish I could forget….

None of the kids in the Baker Street gang is in my class at school. Joey's in the blue group, where all the brainiacs get stuck, and since Mom says I'm about as sharp as a marble, it makes sense I'm in the orange group. I hoped I'd get stuck in the red group with Travis, Emily, and Lily, but nope. I got in orange.

At least I'm not in purple.

"Yeah… I was red. Same as Travis and Lily."

"No shit, Sherlock." Maybe it's still a sore spot for me.

When Emily's lips twist to the side, I know I hurt her feelings.

Even though I want to hug her and say sorry, I roll my eyes like I don't care. Then I shrug as if what I'm going to say next is no big deal. "And, um… Emily, don't mention that princess stuff in front of Travis or Lily, or any of the other guys."

"They'd probably tease him until he cried."

"Yeah, and it wouldn't be pretty." Mom would call this the understatement of the year.

"I'm not gonna say anything, don't worry."

I'm not sure why she thinks I'd worry, but I would. "Good."

"Am I on number thirty?" she asks hopefully.

"You're only on twenty-five, but we can call it thirty if you want."

She laughs and starts counting her sit-ups again at number thirty-one.

9

I END up thinking about Joey a lot when I'm in bed.

Mom's been gone since Saturday morning, and it's Tuesday night. Shit with her and Robby hasn't hit the fan yet, looks like. I'm glad for Mom, but not so much for me. Especially tonight.

I'm no wimp, but I'm a little freaked out on account of the heavy wind. Tree branches keep on scraping against the roof. I been stretched out on my bed with my eyes shut tight, listening to all of the creepy scratching noises for an hour, at least. I'm trying to sleep, but it's an epic fail. And tomorrow our yard's going to be covered in a shit-ton of leaves I should rake, but I probably won't.

An eerie creaking startles me so much I practically bounce out of bed. Once I climb back into my skin, I take a few deep breaths and remind myself that spooky sounds seem spookier when you're alone. And then I try to distract my brain from being scared.

The only thing I want to think about is Joey.

I don't think about at-school Joey because thoughts of him getting pushed around and teased aren't going to help me fall asleep. And I've already run every single one of my memories of him when we were little kids on Baker Street through my brain, like a hundred times each. So I let my mind wander onto how it is when we study together.

I like it best when we're sitting in his living room on the Kinkaids' puffy white couch, drinking all-natural strawberry soda out of glass bottles and talking about the climate regions of the earth. Joey doesn't have his guard up when we're there alone the way he does at school. Neither do I. He turns into this soft,

47

sweet version of himself who's about the smartest guy I know but who doesn't act like he's better than me.

Almost every time we study together, we end up going on "nature walks" to the pump house, and I get to tell Joey everything I know about the outdoors. He listens to me real close, like he's taking notes in his brain on everything I say, and I feel smart. Not in the "I'm a book-smart genius" way like Joey, but in a way that counts too.

I also think about Joey's hair. It's about the prettiest thing I ever seen—smooth and glossy and light. Sometimes I even want to touch it. I'm sure it'd feel like silk between my fingers. I wonder if it still smells sweet, like baby shampoo and bubble gum.

I bet it does.

Nobody but me can ever know I think Joey's hair is nice, though. Not even him. It'd probably hurt his feelings if he knew I think he's pretty, not handsome like a guy's supposed to be.

I curl up in a tight ball and think about how much Joey knows about the topographical surfaces of the earth.

10

I DON'T think my mother lives here anymore.

I have five reasons for thinking this:

Number one is she hasn't been home since last Saturday. All by itself, this is not such a major deal. She's been gone longer before—but it's just my first reason.

Number two is because her blow-dryer is gone. Usually if she's just sleeping over at Robby's house for a night or two, she leaves it here, plugged into the wall in the bathroom. I guess she can get away without it for a few days. But it's *gone* now. I looked for it under the sink and in the linen closet. It's seriously missing. Plus most of her jeans and sweatshirts and socks are missing too. And her underwear.

I'm not supposed to snoop through Mom's drawers—I just happened to notice.

Number three is because of the Fabio book on the kitchen counter. The Fabio book is a paperback book that's got this long-haired muscly dude Mom calls "Fabio" on the cover. Since I was a kid, she's always left a couple of bucks stuck in the middle of it for me in case of an emergency. But now there's *forty freaking dollars* stuck inside the cover. It's like she left more money than usual so I could buy my own pizza and bagels *for weeks*.

Number four's an important reason: after Mom left on Saturday, I found a brand-new cell phone right next to the Fabio book. Not a fancy iPhone or anything, but it's a new phone, and it works. If I press M, Mom's cell phone number pops up. Everybody and their little sister has got a cell phone by eighth grade. Before now, though, whenever I asked for a phone, she said, "Kids don't need cell phones." And now I suddenly do.

Last but certainly not least, as Mom used to say when she lived here, is number five—the note. It says, "Don't wait up for me. I'm gonna be out late." She never left me a note explaining anything before. And Mom's about as late as she can get—she's been gone for four days now.

As far as I can tell, I'm on my own here.

And I'm kind of freaking out.

On the bright side, I can do whatever I want.

So I go into Mom's room and climb up onto her bed, even though I'm still wearing my sneakers. Her sheets don't smell half as bad as mine do. And when I put my head on her pillow, I think I can smell her perfume a little bit. My stupid eyes get wet as I lie here breathing in my mom's smell through my nose, so I do the blinking thing to dry them, but it doesn't work this time. So I wipe my eyes on her pillow, stand up, and jump.

I jump on her bed, hard and fast and angry. I jump on it like I don't care if all the better-smelling-than-mine sheets come flying off or if the mattress springs pop right through and cut my legs and I bleed to death. I jump like I'm going in fast-forward and nothing can stop me. I jump as high as I can and poke at the rough white ceiling with my fingers until little dots of plaster fall on my head and probably look like giant dandruff.

I jump until my eyes aren't even a tiny bit wet anymore, but my hair is sticking to my face with sweat.

I jump until I decide I'm going to go over to Joey's house for a while to study world geography, even though Ms. Paloma didn't give us any geography homework.

I jump right off the bed, thinking Joey's real good at math too.

11

IF I had to rate my friends' houses I go to eat at, I'd say dinner at Travis's house is rock-bottom worst, and dinner at Joey's house when his dad is on a business trip is, by far, the top-dog best. Eating soggy frozen pizza at my house doesn't really count because if you don't eat meat or vegetables or even sit down, it doesn't qualify as real dinner. Lily's family doesn't like me because I'm "almost a street person," according to the grapevine—Lily's parents to Lily to Travis to me—so I never get invited to eat over there. And ranking right in the middle of all the places I eat dinner is Emily's house, which is where I am tonight.

Emily's house is a good place to be. The biggest problem with being here is that her mom is like a mother times ten quadrillion. When I come here, I get treated like a baby—a little bit by Emily—this I'm used to—and a whole lot by Mrs. Monterey. Because of this, right now I'm wearing a pair of Emily's sweatpants and one of her dad's T-shirts.

When I got to their house after soccer practice, Emily and her mom kept on sniffing the air in the kitchen. Emily sniffed the trashcan and then she went over and started sniffing around in the pantry. Mrs. Monterey opened the refrigerator and stuck her nose in, and then off she went to smell the kitty litter box in the corner.

Soon their two freckled noses circled in on me.

"Please don't take offense to this, sweetie, but when was the last time you took a shower?" Emily's mom asked.

That's a tough thing not to take offense to, but I replied, "I showered at school right after practice." I even borrowed Carl Dewey's Old Spice deodorant, so I'm covered in the armpit department too.

"The nasty smell…. Eric, it's coming from you." Emily is always pretty direct, and since I know she isn't being mean, I don't get bent out of shape when she says stuff like this.

"Ouch," I said. I also crossed my eyes to make it funny because Emily's sensitive.

"When did your mother last wash your clothes, dear?" Mrs. Monterey asked.

I couldn't give Mrs. Monterey an honest answer because I can't remember when they last got washed, and I didn't want to lie to a grown-up who's so nice to me. In the end I had to strip down to bare-ass naked and give Emily's mother all my clothes, empty my backpack, and after giving her that, fork over my soccer uniform and my coat so they could all be run through the washer and dryer.

Emily's baby brother keeps saying "Dada" and poking my chest with his chubby finger because I'm wearing his father's favorite Big Papi T-shirt, but I'm okay with this. I like little kids.

"Drop the rest of your laundry off here tomorrow morning before school, honey, and I'll have it washed and folded for you by the time your soccer game is over tomorrow night." Emily's mom calls me lots of mushy pet names. Em says this means she likes me.

"Thank you, ma'am."

Mrs. Monterey is sweet, just the same as Mrs. Kinkaid. But when she says things like "give me all your laundry, you poor, sweet, deprived child" and looks at me with wide, sad eyes, I can feel the pity dripping off her and onto me. Like a thick glob of "I feel sorry for you" honey trickling out of a jar on a high pantry shelf and drizzling all over my face. Getting soaked with that much sticky pity sucks.

We're sitting down together at their round table in their cozy kitchen that always smells like hot apple cider, no matter what's cooking, and we eat a breakfast-food dinner. Scrambled eggs and home fries with sliced red peppers and chocolate chip waffles—not the round frozen kind from a box—and tall glasses of milk, but no bacon because the Montereys don't eat red meat.

Nobody asked for my opinion, but I think Mr. Monterey would make a great dad for me. He's funny and cool and never stops talking about the Boston Red Sox. This is good because all of his chattering about baseball lets me fade into the background and concentrate on eating, even if Toby keeps calling me Dada and I'm wearing Emily's hot-pink sweatpants without any underwear. But thanks to my stupid smelly clothes, Mrs. M keeps bringing the conversation back to Mom and me.

"Is your mother feeding you enough, honey-bun?"

"Yes, ma'am." I'm stuffed full of frozen pizza and bagels on a regular basis.

"I'm really hoping the Sox will pick up a lefty pitcher in the off-season."

"Dada!"

"Because if you are ever hungry, dumplin', you know you can come here for a square meal, right?"

I nod but don't say a word since I'm chewing and it wouldn't be polite, or at least that's my excuse.

"And we're gonna need another good slugger to drive in runs, I'd say."

"Maybe I should call your mother to see if she needs a hand with anything, dear."

I swallow real quick because I have to say, "No—that's kind of a bad idea."

"And why is that?"

"Darlene, just let the boy eat."

"Dada!"

"You look adorable in my sweatpants, Eric."

This is why dinner at Emily's house is nice, but maybe sort of stressful.

And this is why dinner at Emily's house rates right in the middle of the places to eat dinner in Wild Acres.

12

I FLUSH the toilet for what I hope is the last time for a long while and head to the couch to zone out before I start in on my brain-bending homework. As soon as I stretch out on the couch, I put my hands on my belly to feel for gas bubbles and try to figure out if I should eat or not eat. I still feel like shit on wheels, but I probably *should* eat because either my clothes are growing or I'm shrinking. Neither of these options is good.

I think my belly's tied in knots right now because I'm freaking out again. I came close to sticking my nose where it didn't belong today at lunch when Miles Maroney was messing with Joey. I *almost* stuck up for him, but I didn't. In any case, either the fear of what I almost did or the guilt of not doing it is making me sick.

Even if I want to help him, I can't take the risk of being pushed out of my group of friends, because they're basically all I got. But thanks to the whole Joey-Miles "problem," I been on the stupid toilet five times this afternoon. Like I need this right now. It seems every time I get worked up, my belly starts to rumble, and it's TMI to even *think* about what happens next. Today I even had to skip soccer practice on account of my urgent need to…. Like I said, it's TMI.

Truth is, I really wanted to have Joey's back in the cafeteria. When Maroney started mouthing off to him, I curled the fingers of *both* my hands into fists, and I even got out of my chair and took a couple of steps toward them. But when he grabbed Joey by the collar of his shirt and called him a pansy, I chickened out. I didn't want to be called a "pansy-loving flower shop owner," or something like that. And when he clocked Joey upside the head, I hit reverse, and the next thing I knew, my butt was back in my seat, and I was filling my face with the cold meatball sub waiting on my tray. It's a wonder I didn't choke.

In some ways I wish I *did* choke, because I feel so guilty. I deserved to choke.

I'm not proud of how I acted, but I got to be real—I live every day trying to stay out of people's way. Trying to not get noticed. And if I'm going to have a fight with somebody, it ought to be with Mom, not Miles Maroney. *She's* the one who ditched me.

I pretty much have to look at things this way: nothing that happens at school matters enough to get me beat up or suspended and noticed in a way that might get me reported to the powers above, which could get me shipped off to nowhere land.

And what I can't figure out is why Joey wore a pink shirt to school today. Doesn't he have even half a clue? He ought to know that when the *boy* princess of the eighth grade wears pink, there's going to be trouble.

My belly lets out a high-pitched squeak, like the sound that would come out of a monkey's mouth if I tried to bend back its thumbs… if monkeys have thumbs. *Whatever.* The thought of eating frozen pizza again makes me cringe. What I'm craving is meatloaf.

I turn on my side and close my eyes, and my thoughts quickly slide off meatloaf and back onto Joey. He got sent home from school because he barfed after Maroney slugged him in the face, and so he missed World Geography. We learned about the revolution and rotation of the earth. I took careful notes—I tried to write down every single word that came out of Ms. Paloma's mouth, even though it was like Greek to me. I'll stop by the Kinkaids' house later tonight when I'm sure my belly isn't going to pull a fast one, and if he lets me in, he can copy down my notes. It'll be sort of like making up for just sitting there and watching him get clocked today at lunch. And maybe if he's up for it, he can explain my notes to me.

I sure hope Joey's not too mad to let me back into his house. Maybe it's time I taught him how to fight, seeing as I'm a lousy personal bodyguard.

WHEN I knock on their front door, Mrs. Kinkaid answers, and right away I can tell she's been crying. I feel more like a worm than I did before, and I'm kind of surprised this is possible.

"Um, is Joey… like, okay enough to see me?"

"He's sleeping, Eric, and I don't want to wake him until his father comes home. Mr. Kinkaid is flying in from Chicago tonight."

Usually I don't stop by here when Joey's not expecting me because anybody's mom could drive by with their kid in the passenger seat and see me standing on the doorstep of the "princess's castle." But tonight I *had* to come. I needed to make sure Joey was alive.

"Okay, I guess," I say, and then I sling my backpack off my shoulder and unzip it. "Could you give my notebook to Joey? Since I'm his study buddy, I took extra good notes in World Geography so he could copy them down." I hold it out to her.

She smiles at me like I'm some kind of hero, and when she takes the notebook out of my hand, I swear a knife stabs into my heart and then heads south to carve out my gut.

Guilt sucks.

"You are such a thoughtful friend, Eric. Of course I'll tell him. Wait right here for a second." Mrs. Kinkaid rushes down the hall, and I look around to see if any cars I recognize are driving by on Baker Street.

When she comes back and hands me a plastic baggie filled with brownies, I want to say, "No, thank you, I don't deserve these," but I keep my mouth shut. I just take them from her, turn around, and book it down the stairs before I get caught here.

13

JOEY COMES back to school with a puffy black eye and a more timid than before attitude. The teachers hover around him, but this just makes Joey's black eye and new fear more obvious. It makes what is bad so much worse.

Miles Maroney gets suspended from school for three days, and even though he deserved much more than that, I hope that other kids will still get the message—keep your paws off Joey Kinkaid.

I pass by Joey in the hallway three times before geography class, but he never lifts his eyes off the floor to look at me. Not that we'd actually say hi to each other in public, because we wouldn't, but we know how to say stuff to each other using just our eyes. In World Geography, though, he's *got* to look at me. After all, he needs to thank me for lending him my notebook.

When time for geography class finally comes, I sit down beside him at our pushed-together desks, and Joey says, "Thanks for dropping your notebook at my house last night, Eric." He looks at me, and I get caught up in staring at the dark-purple bruise surrounding his pretty blue eye. "I copied everything down."

"It was no problem. I wanted to see you, but your mom said you were sleeping." I can't stop gawking at his black eye—it looks so wrong on his smooth pale skin.

"After the doctor said I didn't have a concussion, Mom let me sleep all afternoon until Dad got home."

"Well, I think the whole thing sucks, you know?" I'm the official King of Lame because saying this is all I'm willing to do to fix it.

Joey nods. "If you want to come by Saturday, we can talk about revolution and rotation."

"Okay. And I was thinking maybe we can talk about you learning how to throw a punch." I can't believe I'm actually planning to go through with this, but if I'm not going to stand up for Joey, at least I can teach him to stand up for himself.

For the first time probably since yesterday before he barfed, Joey smiles. It makes me feel good, so I do a few fake fighting moves to see if I can get his smile to last. It works, and I feel like a brave knight even though I'm much more of a low-down coward.

SATURDAY MORNING fighting practice doesn't go very well. Joey just isn't into it, and he can't focus. He keeps doing dance moves in the grass. I can relate because I'm not too focused in Health and Family Living class, and my mind always wanders to WWE moves. So after an hour of him doing the boot scootin' boogie instead of boxing moves in his backyard, I change my plan. "Maybe instead of throwing a punch, you should just run like the wind when somebody gets that look in his eye."

"What look?" Joey asks after he performs a near-perfect triple twirl.

The kid has got to be clueless. "The look like he's itching to punch your lights out."

Joey pulls the elastic band off the top of his head, and silky blond hair spills all over his shoulders. I almost ask him if I can have the elastic band because my hair's the longest it's ever been, and I'd love to take off my itchy brown beanie and somehow still keep my hair out of my eyes. But the last thing I need is a damn ponytail. So instead I watch as he flicks his hair off his shoulders like he used to do when he was the Little Mermaid.

"There's times you gotta run like your life depends on it— see what I'm saying?" I ask.

I don't think he likes my question, because he doesn't answer. "Let's go for a walk," he suggests and takes off toward the path. Joey's real good at distraction too.

I have this weird feeling that he wants to shout "Chase me!" like he did way back when, but he stays quiet. I still do it, though—I run after him. Like two little kids, we race down the path, kicking our feet through the clumps of new-fallen leaves scattered on the ground.

Joey runs right to the edge of the pond beside the pump house, and then he comes to a screeching halt. I almost run into his back, and when he turns around to look at me, we're practically on top of each other. He's just about as tall as I am, so our eyes are close to level. Even though I make it a rule to never look at him too direct, I go and break my own rule. And when I do, I see eyes that are clear and blue—bluer than the ice-cold sky on the morning after a snowstorm, and maybe even bluer than a robin's egg that's fallen out of the nest and is resting all helpless in the grass. My fingers find the upside-down purple moon shape underneath his right eye, which kind of breaks new ground in our non-friendship. I touch it softly and shake my head.

"I hate that he hit you." Then my hand slides down to cup the whole side of his face. I gasp at my own action; my hand is doing what it wants without my brain's permission.

"Dad said Miles hit me because I'm too much like a girl."

"He shouldn't punch girls either."

"Dad's right. I *am* like a girl."

I let my hand drop to my side and take a step back. And this time I *really* look at Joey. Maybe he's not wearing his mother's purple sundress, but he's dressed more like Emily and Lily than Travis and me. I'm wearing dirty jeans and a dirtier T-shirt with probably the dirtiest sweatshirt in the whole town of Wild Acres over it, and a snug, sweaty beanie pulled low over my ears to hold my hair down. Joey's wearing a sweatshirt too, but it's bright aqua and says *American Eagle* across the front in sewed-on white letters. And I think you call the kind of pants he's wearing "leggings." The girls at school wear them almost every day with the same kind of furry boots he's got on.

"I feel like one," he says softly.

"Damn it," I reply. I don't say "What do you mean? You feel like *what*?" I know exactly what he means. I know how he feels because it's who he is—or at least, it's how I see him. Being more like a girl than a boy is just Joey, and it's always been Joey, and I don't mind it. *But why the hell do we have to talk about it?* Time to shut this conversation down. "Whatever, Joe."

Standing at the edge of the pond, Joey looks down at the ground and off to the side. I'm pretty sure I hurt his feelings by being rude. I didn't really mean to; I just don't want to talk about how he feels like a girl, because this isn't just about him. It's also about *me*. It's about how I think about him when I lie in bed at night, and certain feelings I get even though I don't want them. And it's about how less than one minute ago, I looked into his eyes and thought they were beautiful, and then I reached up to touch his face because I couldn't not. It's about how I've wanted to stick my nose in his hair since I was six years old.

"Your dad doesn't know anything." When I scrape the back of my brain for the right words, my nose is probably scrunched up like I'm the most clueless human being in ten square miles. "You're just a different kind of guy, that's all."

He shifts his eyes in my direction, and I get locked up in his gaze. In his eyes I see an expression I'm not used to—a cross between miserable and panicked and "I'm gonna lose it." "Something's *wrong* with me, Eric. I mean, everybody *says* I'm a boy, but it just doesn't *feel* right to me"

"Damn it," I say again because this is a messed-up subject... plus nothing's wrong with him.

And then Joey does the strangest thing ever. He spins around and charges into the pond.

"What the heck are you doing, Joe?" I call after him.

But he doesn't stop—he walks as fast as the water will let him, and soon he's up to his waist in the sludgy, weedy pond.

"Get out of there! The pond's dirty, and it's cold out and— just come back here!" It's nuts for him to be standing in a muddy pond in the middle of October. And next thing I know, Joey's up to his shoulders—this is when I get kind of scared. He isn't swimming around; he's stuck in one place like he's hoping the pond will swallow him up.

I can't just stand here and watch him drown, so I rush into the water after him. The splash I make when I jump into the pond catches his attention. As stiff as a robot, Joey turns around and says, "Stop, Eric—I'm gonna come out." His eyes are dark and empty—not robin's-egg blue anymore—and even if his purplish-blue lips are telling me something else, the way he's staring past me begs "Please just leave me here."

As he trudges out of the water, Joey looks over my left shoulder and into the woods. I don't check behind me to see who's there because I know he's just fixing his eyes on a rock or a tree— on anything but me. Once he's standing beside me on the mud, he spreads his fragile fingers over his face, as if he can hide there, and then starts shivering like a puppy after a bath.

I'm only wet up to my knees. My sneakers are probably toast, but at least I'm not half-frozen. I know I got to do something, so I bark, "Arms up."

He obediently takes his fingers off his face and lifts his arms, and just like he's a little kid, I pull his soaking sweatshirt up and over his head. I'm shocked, but somehow *not* shocked, at what I see underneath—a purple lacy bra-thing on his pale skinny chest. I don't try to take it off, even though it's drenched too. I just yank off my own sweatshirt, and, hoping it doesn't smell like the back end of a donkey, I pull it right over his head. "We got to get you home before you turn into a Popsicle."

Joey nods, but I have a feeling his mind isn't here on the muddy edge of the pump house pond anymore. And it hits me hard—he knows I just learned his biggest secret—that somewhere, not too deep inside the boy Joey, really *is* a girl. But I always had a feeling about it, even if it wasn't spelled out like it is now.

"Your mom is at the mall, right?" I try to get our minds back on business.

"Uh-huh."

"And your dad's away on a business trip?"

I get a blank-faced nod.

I'm pretty sure Joey can get back into his house without anybody knowing what he just did. I'll take his muddy soaking-wet clothes back to my house in a grocery bag and, for him, I'll finally get off my ass and figure out how the washing machine works. I can put his dirty stuff in with some stuff of my own, and then smuggle his clothes back into his dresser drawers some night when we're supposed to be studying. But I'll have to wear last year's too-tight sneakers until this year's sneakers dry out on my back porch.

So I got the details covered, but as far as the big picture goes, my best bet is probably to pretend this never happened, because who wants to accept that his World Geography study buddy just tried to drown himself in the pump house pond?

"I can fix this for you. It'll be like it never happened."

Joey nods. And I got no clue why, but I find myself staring at his chin and studying the tremors as his teeth chatter together. I guess maybe his chin is a safer zone to look at than his wide, dry eyes or his sad, quivering lips.

I fake a laugh and say, "I'm not sure what made you think today would be a good day for a swim, Joe."

He doesn't even smile, and he's the kind of guy to smile when he's supposed to. I don't know much about much, but I know that something is very wrong.

When I reach out one arm and stick it around his shoulder, it's like he turns into Play-Doh. He molds himself against me. We stand here close together, and I share the heat from my body with him. Real gradual, his shivering stops. And even though it's kind of messed-up, I feel strong and smart, like I'm some kind of hero.

Like I'm Joey's hero.

"Come on, man. Let's get you home." Side by side, with my arm still hanging around his shoulders, we walk back down the pump house path toward his house. I stay quiet even though I want to ask him if he was *really* trying to be gone from the world, because it sure seemed that way. More than anything, I want to beg Joey to *please* never pull a stunt like that again, because even though I haven't ever told him, he's the only person in this entire world who makes me feel like I'm not alone on that window ledge.

Joey's out on the ledge right beside me.

And thanks to the way everybody's gawking at *him*—at his long hair and his pink shirt and the way he floats instead of walks—they don't notice I'm getting ready to jump too.

14

I HAVEN'T stopped by Joey's house after school for the past few days, and I don't stop by today either. What happened Saturday was just too messed-up for me to deal with. Plus I been worrying 24-7, and I'm no doctor, but I think I need a break from it. And going home and sitting alone in front of the TV isn't the kind of break I need, because doing that just makes me wonder if I'm ever going to see Mom again. I've pretty much given up on her since I left, like, four voicemail messages on her phone saying I wouldn't mind eating pizza with her some night, and she never called me back.

The decision to skip soccer practice is a little bit harder than usual today because it means I won't get to play in the game tomorrow. But Coach Petrassi doesn't make me feel like I'm a needed part of the team, so it isn't a huge loss. During practice yesterday, he looked at me with a frown, shook his head, and muttered something like, "So much wasted potential." Last week he told me it's "a crying shame" that I can't get my act together enough to make it to practice every day. But he's got no freaking clue about *my act*.

Coach Petrassi hasn't got a clue about what it's like to live on frozen pizza and water from the kitchen sink, or to wear clothes that smell like the barnyard because you fell asleep instead of doing laundry. And I'm not about to let Emily's mom do my laundry seeing as she'll ask me questions about why the hell my own mother doesn't care that my clothes stink to high heaven—that's no fun either. I bet Coach Petrassi couldn't say "been there, done that" if he knew how lately I been talking to myself around the house because I'm so frigging lonely.

Nope. Coach Clueless has no idea.

So today I'm going to go to a bright place where people are. Where they got healthy snacks like carrots and yogurt dip and hot cocoa in tiny cups, and there are little kids playing and happy moms chattering. *And* there are lots of books too, but they aren't the reason I used to go to the Wild Acres Public Library every Wednesday afternoon until I joined the soccer team.

When I got home from school today, I sniffed all the clothes I keep in balls on my bedroom floor and picked out the ones that smell most like nothing. When I go to the library on Wednesday afternoons, I sit *right* next to the little kids, so I can't smell like a petting zoo. Now I'm on my bike, peddling as fast as I can because the Mom and Tot Playgroup starts in ten minutes, and it takes fifteen minutes to ride my bike downtown.

As soon as I get to the library, I hide my wheels in the bushes with a strong hope that nobody swipes it, because if they do, there goes my transportation. I pull my beanie down low on my head and push my too-long hair up inside it so I don't look like Tarzan to the moms, and then I run into the library and take a quick right to the stairs that lead down to the basement where the kids' room is.

"Eric!" Little Misty sees me first, and she runs right over and hugs me around my legs.

"Hi, Misty. How's kindergarten?" I ask.

"Good. I like snack time and finger painting best," she replies, looking up at me with big brown eyes that make me melt every time.

"Eric's here!" she yells.

"You guys, Eric came!" Little voices that sound like they just sucked on a bunch of helium balloons pipe up all around me.

"Can I sit on your lap when you read the story?" Jack asks. He always makes sure to ask first so I can't say no.

"Hi, Harry… and sure, Jack, you can sit on my lap. Hey, I don't know your name, little dude."

"He's Jeffrey, and it's his first day at playgroup."

The kids crowd around me, and it feels good because they think I'm something. I mess up all of their hair, one by one, and wink at them a few times each, and finally they go back to playing with Legos. Today they're building castles on wheels, which is such a cool idea that I want to know who thought it up. I figure it was probably Jan, who's in charge here. I look over at the moms and send them my best smile. And I wave too, but I do it real casual.

"Hello, Eric. We've missed you so much over the past few weeks," says Mrs. Allen. She's the youngest mom here and has a sweet, shy smile. She always looks right at me and nods when I say something, even if it's dumb. I like her the best, but I still treat all the mothers exactly the same so nobody's feelings get hurt.

"Hi, Mrs. Allen. I miss you guys too, but it's soccer season, and I got to go to practice, or I can't play in the games."

"Of course you should go to practice, but we want you to know that the kids have asked about you every Wednesday." Misty's mom likes to be called Tammy instead of Mrs. Johnson. She's a lot older than Mrs. Allen, and she also has a bunch of big kids who go upstairs to the adult part of the library and do homework while Misty is in playgroup. Tammy always looks tired. I can relate.

I say my hellos to the other moms—even to Jack's grandma, who always dumps him off where the other kids are playing and then goes and sits alone in the corner of the kids' room with a magazine and a cup of coffee from Dunkin' Donuts. I can tell that sometimes she closes her eyes, even though she tries to make it look like she's reading a magazine. I never say a word to her about this because it sucks if you think you got found out when you're hiding something.

"Look at my castle-mobile, Eric!" one of the kids calls, and I head right back to the play rug.

I take turns rolling each of the kid's castle-mobiles along the counter beside the window, and I make a big deal out of how cool they are and how fast they go. Harry's castle loses a wheel when I roll it down a tilted picture book, but I stick it back on before anybody sees.

"Now *you* make one!" Harry demands, so I sit down on the rug, and all the kids gather around me and watch as I make a castle with towers and a built-in moat. I even swipe a tiny plastic dragon from the toy box and stick it inside.

"Now, Jeffrey, can you find me some wheels and help me put 'em on the bottom of my castle?" I pick Jeffrey as my helper because he looks lost and alone, and I know that feeling. It isn't good.

"Sure I will, Eric." He smiles at me wide—I see a big hole where a front tooth used to be—before he scrambles off to find some wheels.

"I'll bet the tooth fairy visited your house last week," I add, and again he grins.

I'm pretty sure I just made another friend.

"Eric, when you're finished building your castle-mobile, come on over and take a look at the book you're going to read to the children."

Janice Winston is the children's librarian at the Wild Acres Public Library. I wish my teachers at school could be like her. She thinks I'm smart enough to read a book to a whole group of little kids *and* to talk about it afterward. She always says stuff like, "Nice job with your reading expression" and "Someday, children, you'll be able to read as well as Eric," and I feel like a rock star.

Once Jeffrey has stuck the wheels on my rolling castle, I tell the kids they can play with it before story time. They fight over who gets it first, which makes me even prouder.

"Today, Eric, you're going to read *The Knight and the Dragon* by Tomie dePaola. Here you go." She hands me a hardcover book with a huge friendly looking dragon on the front and a cute little knight beside him. It makes me think of all the times Joey and me played Princess and Knight....

"You're my knight in shining armor, Sir Eric, and you must do my bidding." Mrs. Kinkaid reads lots of storybooks to Princess, so she knows how royal people talk for real. "I need four white mushrooms and a bunch of tiny flowers, only purple ones, and lots of sticks... because today we are building a bridge from here to Terabithia."

"'Kay."

"You're supposed to say, 'Yes, my fair princess.'"

"Oh, yeah." And I'm also supposed to kneel down when I "address royalty." I guess I forgot again. So I get down on my knees in the grass in front of her and bow my head and say it right. "Yes, my fair princess."

"You may go in search of the wilderness treasures, my bravest knight. But beware of fire-breathing dragons." She touches my forehead with her fingertips. "Fare ye well, Sir Eric of Wild Acres."

I get onto my feet real fast and run into the woods to look for the stuff she wants to build the bridge to... to wherever that place is. The flowers are super easy to find. I have to try a lot harder to find mushrooms, and finally I see two fat white ones on the edge of the pump house path.

Just two of them.

"Crap-tastic," I say the made-up swear word under my breath. And I want to look for more mushrooms, but I can't keep the princess waiting all day 'cause she'll worry I got burned into toast by a fire-breathing dragon. So I run deeper into the woods and collect a big pile of sticks. To make up for not having enough mushrooms, I pick up six of the early fall leaves that dropped to the ground. And I choose perfect ones. Bright yellow, like Princess's hair. Then I run back to her.

"Present your gifts, my knight," my princess says. Her voice sounds grown-up.

I kneel down like I'm supposed to and put the flowers and the mushrooms and the sticks and the leaves on the grass between us.

When I bow my head, Princess says, "You have failed me."

My eyes get wet so fast I can't stop it.

"But worry not, you have still pleased me." She touches the underneath part of my chin, and I figure it's okay to look up at her. "And I have a special idea for what to do with the golden leaves."

Once I know she's not mad, I wipe my eyes and take a big breath, and it's okay again. Then we squat down next to each other, and I watch as Princess builds a beautiful bridge to a faraway fantasyland, with sticks for the sides and golden leaves for the roof and the floor. Before she puts on the roof, though, she lets me sprinkle purple flower petals to make a safe sidewalk for us to walk on so we don't get hit by a horse-drawn carriage. When I'm done, she sticks a mushroom guard at each end.

And then she smiles.

"Why don't you flip through the book to see if you are comfortable with it?"

I'm so deep in thought I jump a little when Jan speaks to me, but I snap back to reality pretty quick. What Jan means is she wants me to make sure I know all the words so I can read them out loud and not embarrass myself. "Thanks, Jan." She's so cool.

I check out the book and realize right away from the illustrations that I've read other stuff by this dude before. "Didn't I read a book called *Strega Nona* by this same writer?" I ask.

"Wow, yes! I'm impressed that you made the connection."

My face gets hot, but it's in the good way.

"Please call the children to the story corner when you're ready, Eric."

There are about ten beanbag chairs in the story corner. When I announce, "It's story time," castles and wheels go flying, and all the kids scramble to get their favorite color beanbag chair. Shit like the color chair you plant your butt on matters a lot to kids.

"What's wrong, Misty?" I ask because her bottom lip is poking out.

"I wanted to sit on a yellow beanbag chair."

"Hmmm. I wonder what we can do to make Misty happy again." I say it loud so everybody hears.

Jeffrey slides to the side of the huge yellow beanbag. "There's room for you beside me, Misty."

"That's a super great idea. You guys can *share* the yellow one." I'm pretty good with kids; the library moms say so every time I help out with playgroup.

Once I'm sitting on the gray beanbag, the only one left, Jack climbs onto my lap, and I read the story. A long time ago, Jan showed me how to read the words on a page and then turn the book around, nice and high, so all the kids can see the picture. Jack helps me hold up the book. Seeing his chubby little fingers on the bottom of the book in between my big hands makes my eyes get wet—I got no clue why—and I blink away wetness every time we turn the page.

Everybody knows that when the story is over, it's time for snacks. I try to walk real slow over to the snack table, but it's hard because I'm so hungry. Mrs. Allen lets me have *four* tiny cups of hot cocoa and extra carrots and dip.

My heart sinks when the mothers start pulling their kids' coats from the hooks on the wall because I know that the Mom and Tot Playgroup is almost over, and I'm going to be alone again. I have to swallow like ten times in a row to make the stupid lump in my throat get small enough not to choke me.

Before everybody takes off, I collect lots of hugs, and when the kids stick their noses right into my belly, I'm glad I took the time to find a T-shirt that doesn't stink too bad.

Jan is the last one to say goodbye to me. "So, Eric, is everything going okay in your life these days?" She stands behind the snack table, studying me. So I study her right back; it's my best defense. Jan always dresses like she's ready to hike up a mountain. She's got on dark-green pants with a huge cargo pocket on her right thigh that could hold enough granola bars to last a guy all day, and a tan shirt that somebody's dad might wear fly-fishing. Jan isn't the makeup kind of lady, and she wears her hair long and straight and flat. She is a very no-frills person.

I sure wish I could tell her the truth. "Things are great." Lucky I know how to lie real good.

She pulls a gallon-sized Ziploc bag out from under the box on the table and fills it up with leftover carrots and apple slices, and then she puts the plastic cover tight on the bowl of dip. "Just bring the bowl back the next time you come to playgroup, okay?"

"Thanks, Jan." Most kids I know start drooling when they see chocolate cupcakes. How messed-up is it that I salivate when I look at baby carrots?

"And take care of yourself, Eric. Remember, if you need anything, I'm here almost every afternoon." Jan's dark-brown eyes are always steady. When she looks at me real direct, I get a safe feeling I'm not used to. For a split second, I wonder what it would be like if she was my mom.

Damn it! That stupid lump fills up my whole throat, and I can't even say goodbye to her. I know it's lame, but all I can do is wave on my way to the stairs.

15

IT STARTS up again in World Geography class.

"Um, Joey, did you steal my boots? Because I've got a pair just like that in my bedroom closet?" Lily looks at Travis, and he smiles at her like she did a good thing by being a mean piss-ant.

"My pansy alarm is sounding louder right now than ever before in history. It's a day for the record books, right, Eric?"

Joey has a new pair of furry boots since he ruined his other pair in the pond when he tried to drown himself last Saturday. I wonder how he explained his ruined UGGs to Mrs. Kinkaid. "Save it, Jenkins," I shoot back, trying to make it sound halfhearted. I cough to distract him and then focus on my handout.

Things were messed up last weekend when Joey charged into the pond with all his clothes on, and it's getting less normal at school with Joey too. This is mostly because instead of wearing those crisp tan pants and plain white sneakers every day, he's been wearing tight black leggings and furry boots, just like the girls wear.

Luckily he still comes to school in his regular Grandpa-looking collared shirts, but now he doesn't button them, and he wears a clingy tank top underneath. I have no clue how he expects kids to react when they see him dressed up like a girl. Nobody asked me, but I think he sets himself up to get teased and beat on.

Travis and Lily won't lay off him.

"Hey, Josie, I'll meet you behind the Sinking Stone Mall after school. I promise, after I beat you silly, I'll take you shopping for *boys'* clothes." Travis's unibrow sinks low over his eyes.

"Maybe if you behave, we'll let you get your hair dyed pink at the Mall Makeover Beauty Salon before you go home."

Lily laughs and then twirls a few strands of her shiny black hair around a finger. "Hot pink hair would work on Joey. Don't you think, Travis?"

"On *Josie*," Travis corrects her and grins.

Joey sits beside me, his hands covering his face.

And maybe I don't stick up for Joey very well, but I don't throw him under the bus either. "Shut up, you guys. Ms. Paloma's looking at us." We're supposed to be reading a handout about life on a Native American reservation, not discussing Joey's hair.

"When did you turn into such a kiss ass, Sinclair?" Travis asks.

"When he became BFFs with the gayest geek at school," Lily says, then looks at Travis to collect another smile.

"Travis, Lily, Eric, and Joey—are you four interested in spending some quality time with me after school?" Ms. P calls across the room, and then she folds her arms like she means business.

Joey, who didn't glance away from his handout the whole time he was getting tag-teamed by his old Baker Street pals, looks up at Ms. Paloma and squeaks, "Sorry, Ms. Paloma."

Joey would do better to get a detention and act like a normal kid for an hour after school. And since he reads faster than the rest of us, he slides his handout to the side of his desk and pulls out a book about a hitchhiker and the solar system from his backpack. I wish he was telling me about that book instead of reading it to himself.

Actually I wish I could be anywhere but here.

Travis waits a couple of minutes and then starts whispering across the aisle to me again. "Halloween is Friday night. Are we gonna go out trick-or-treating around the neighborhood or what?"

"I guess so," I whisper back. There's no one at home to stop me by lecturing that I'm too old to trick-or-treat.

"Cool. I'm gonna buy a couple dozen eggs." He cracks a sideways smile and looks down at the papers on his table before Ms. Paloma has a chance to give us detention.

I REFUSE to egg the Kinkaids' house. It's like there's a line in the sand that I just won't cross. I eat dinner here three times a week. *How can I throw eggs at the place?*

Now it's past midnight and, for the most part, Halloween is a done deal. And maybe *my* mother doesn't care what I do or where I sleep or if I sleep at all, but Travis's folks *say* they do. He told Chuckie and Mrs. Jenkins he's sleeping at my house, which means we don't exactly have to be anywhere, so we're still lurking around the neighborhood in the pitch-blackness.

Surprise, surprise—not! We end up in front of Joey's house.

"What's happening to you, Sinclair? You're turning into a total wimp, just like Princess Josie." Travis is mad at me again, but I just shrug because I'm not up for a fistfight.

Emily and Lily came along with us trick-or-treating tonight. They concocted their own fake sleepover plans so they can stay out all night too. The four of us are dressed like baseball players in Mr. Monterey's Red Sox jerseys and ball caps, which is lame, but it got the job of "find a costume" done so the parents would give us candy when we knocked at their doors. None of us said "trick or treat," though. We're way too old for that kind of thing.

Lily asks, "Why are you such a baby lately, Eric?"

Travis steps up to me and sticks an egg in my hand. "Go ahead—chuck it."

Combined, Travis and Lily have already pitched a dozen eggs at Mrs. Kinkaid's silver Volvo wagon and the chalk-white front door of their house. The empty egg carton is upside-down on the sidewalk, and I'm standing next to it—crouched down and half-hidden by a mini-Christmas tree—and gawking at Joey's house like I never seen a yellow building with four walls and a roof before.

The stress of being pressured so hard makes time stand still… and my mind does the spacing-out thing it's so good at.

The egg in my hand makes me think of birds, and the thought of birds brings me back to second grade when we pretended we were birds almost every day at recess. My head escapes there for a few minutes....

I can feel my nose crunching up when I look at Joey. I don't want to look dopey, so I try hard to un-wrinkle it. "Why did Mrs. Robinson say you can't be a fairy princess... and that we all have to be birds?" I ask.

Joey shakes his head. I don't think he likes my question much. Instead of answering, he declares in a loud voice, "I'm the Swan Princess."

Emily kicks at the playground dirt with the toe of her shiny black shoe. "Why do you get to be the Swan Princess?"

Joey doesn't answer her question either. "What kind of bird are you?" he asks, looking right at me. But I don't know what kind of bird I'm gonna be until I hear what everybody else is gonna be.

"Caw! Caw!" In a booming bird voice, Travis tells us what we already figured out. "I'm a crow! Caw! Caw!" When he jumps off his nest and flaps his wings, I know he's ready to fly.

"I'm going to be a hummingbird," Emily tells us.

Joey smiles. That was a good choice.

"I'm a bald eagle, and I eat other birds." Lily shakes her head slowly, as if she's sad that she's gonna have to eat us, but I think she's glad.

Everybody looks at me, but I still haven't got any ideas, so I shrug.

The Swan Princess says, "You are a seagull, Eric." She says it real firm and serious, like a seagull is an important bird. And then she flaps her feathery, silver wings and flies high up into the sky, followed close behind by a tiny hummingbird, a cawing crow, a hungry bald eagle, and an important seagull.

Back in elementary school, we never switched our bird roles around—Joey was *always* the Swan Princess—it was like a rule. And the only problem with pretending we were birds was when Travis turned into a crow, he was super annoying and wouldn't stop cawing unless I paid him a quarter.

"Didn't you hear me? I told you to chuck it!" Travis's voice brings me back to real life, where I'm crouched on the sidewalk with an egg in my hand, looking through the dark at Joey's majestic house, with Travis and Lily and Emily watching me to see what I'm going to do. Like they're my judge and jury, Mom would say if she'd stuck around.

Lucky for me Emily has more common sense than the rest of us all put together. "I'm out of here. If my mother finds out I egged a house, I'll be grounded until eighth-grade graduation." She starts to walk away but stops. "Are you coming with me, Eric?"

So much stuff goes through my mind in the next second or two I can hardly sort through it all: Number one is I *always* do what Travis tells me to do. And Lily—she'll never let me hear the end of it if I wimp out. Number two is lately Mrs. Kinkaid's been more of a mom to me than Mom has. How can I chuck eggs at her stuff when she treats me so good?

But number three is the big one—it's Joey. I get a picture in my head of him opening the front door in the morning and seeing the mess we made of his house and his car and…. I drop the egg on the sidewalk, turn around, and catch up with Emily, calling back to Travis and Lily, "I don't need to get arrested tonight, thank you very much!"

"You wuss!" Travis yells. An egg smashes near my feet on the sidewalk. "And you owe me an egg!"

"Get a life, Eric!" Lily calls after me. I hear the sound of the mailbox opening. "Check out my aim, Travis—I bet yah I can throw an egg *into* the Kinkaids' mailbox from across the street."

"Oh yeah? Prove it!" They aren't even trying to be quiet. I glance around for blue lights, but don't see any.

As we walk away, I hear hoots and hollers and eggs smashing on metal. Lily and Travis are probably destroying the Kinkaids' cheerful mailbox with the yellow house painted on the side. I'm as mad as hell, and I have to grit my teeth so I don't scream.

"Come on, Emily—let's get outta here!" I loud-whisper.

Emily and me start to run, but every time I hear the sound of an egg crashing against the mailbox, it makes my guts twist up into a bowl of cooked spaghetti.

EMILY ENDS up staying at my house. We grab my pillow and Mom's pillows, and all of the blankets off my bed, and then we set up a nest on the living room floor.

"Where's your mother?" she asks.

I keep my face as blank as I can so I don't give my secret away. "She's down in Rhode Island tonight, visiting my grandma." Lying is so easy lately.

"Your mother let you stay here *by yourself?*" I look at Emily and admit to myself that she's sort of pretty. Not pretty the way Joey is—her hair is straight and plain brown like mine, and her eyes don't glow the way his do—but her freckles are cute, and she has a goodness about her that shows when she smiles. Not that she's smiling right now, because she's not. Her mouth is gaping open, and she's gawking at me like I'm a porcupine in a balloon factory.

"I… you know, I told Mom that Travis was sleeping over. So she didn't think I'd be here all alone."

"Staying here with Travis and no grown-up to supervise you guys is worse than you staying here alone." Emily looks at me strangely, and I wonder if she believes Mom is *really* off visiting Grandma for the night.

But Emily's *so* right about staying here alone with Travis being kind of unsafe. He's bound to do anything. "Well, I'm not alone. You're here, right?"

"*My* mother would freak if she knew I was sleeping over at a boy's house." Finally Emily smiles. "But she thinks I'm with Lily, and Lily's parents think she's with me, so I guess it's all good."

"No harm, no foul," I say because it sounds cool, even though I haven't got a clue what the expression's supposed to mean.

"Yeah." Emily yawns and curls into the blankets. I turn on the TV like I always do lately when I'm trying to fall asleep, even though we're both too tired to watch. It's nice not to sleep here alone for once. And Emily's much better company than just the TV.

"Why do Travis and Lily hate Joey so much?" I ask her. I'm usually not the one to bring up stuff like this because it's complicated, and I'm not, but I ask anyhow.

"I guess they hate him because he's different." Her voice sounds sleepy.

"Do *you* hate him, Em?" I'm not sure why, but I need to know where Emily stands on this.

"No. I have no reason to hate Joey. He's gotten really shy since we started middle school, so I don't hang around with him anymore."

I nod, but Emily isn't looking. I can see from the light of the late show on TV that her eyes are closed.

"Do *you* hate him?" she asks and yawns again.

This time I shake my head, but she's already asleep.

16

"I'M NOT saying I'm freezing to death or anything, Mom, but it's no fun to take a shower in ice-cold water."

"I told you I'd pay the electric company as soon as I have a second. But I've been watching Robby's kids pretty much around the clock, and they don't give me a moment of peace to get on the computer and pay bills."

I sigh loud enough for Mom to hear. "I won't be able to cook my pizza or see at night until the electricity is back on. How am I supposed to do my homework?"

"Lighten up, Eric. The world isn't coming to an end. It's just the electricity, not the Black Death."

I'm actually kind of impressed that Mom knows about the historic plague I studied in sixth-grade social studies class, but I'm not in the mood to give her props. "So when are you going to email the electric company, Mom?"

"When I have a minute. That's when." She ends the call.

"I guess I won't hold my breath," I mutter to nobody and stick the phone into the back pocket of my too-loose jeans.

As I shuffle over to the bus, I decide to look at the bright side of a depressing situation. At least the electricity didn't go off on Halloween night when Emily was sleeping over because it would've probably freaked *both* of us out. We'd have figured that pissed-off Halloween ghosts followed us home from Joey's house and did it, and our lives were in serious jeopardy.

But last night I kind of *did* flip out when it all of a sudden got pitch-black and deathly silent in my living room. I'm a guy who wants to fix things, though. So as soon as I figured out that the electricity just got shut off and the world wasn't coming to an end, my brain shifted into action mode, and I tried to figure out what the heck I was going to do next. All I could come up with was to worry my butt off, seeing as I figured calling Mom in the middle of the night wasn't going to do any good.

So this seems to be my genius plan: I'm going to worry my butt off....

I need hot water to take showers with... and the toaster to make my bagels... and the oven for my frozen pizzas... and light 'cause it gets dark early now, and I got a pile of homework every night... and it's getting cold outside too, so I'm gonna need some heat or I'll turn into a Popsicle when I'm asleep and....

Last night, after I chewed my fingernails off, I worried myself to sleep, but I managed to get off to school okay. For the record, cold showers bite. A bagel isn't too bad if it's not toasted, as long as you smother it in peanut butter and fluff. The thing is, my milk and OJ, and the pizzas in the freezer, are going to get rotten if the electricity doesn't get turned back on today.

I'm sitting here in the front seat of the bus, across from where Joey's sitting, and am not messing around with Travis or Lily or Emily. I steer clear of everybody. When it's time to think hard, it's best for me to do it alone.

After a few seconds of deep thinking, I decide I was lucky for two reasons last night when the electricity went off: number one is that my phone was charged, which was good in case the cottage started to burn down and I needed to call 911. And number two is that in the back of the top shelf of the fridge, we had the right size batteries for the flashlight I found on the back steps.

I did my homework by the glow of the flashlight, and I didn't start to feel like a human Popsicle until I was standing naked, one foot in and one foot out of the shower this morning, trying to wash my privates with water as cold as a mountain stream.

I hate to get all worked up about things I can't control, but lately I just can't help it. I know the facts—if Mom's late putting money in the Fabio book, I'll go hungry. And now I've got to worry every month that she's going to space out and forget to pay the electric bill. Cable TV—well, that's long gone, but with electricity, I could get a few staticky channels to keep me company at night. At least she's all paid up on my cell phone, so I can call for help in the case of an emergency. But I get this sick feeling that the bottom's going to drop out of this whole Eric-lives-alone thing, and I'll end up who knows where.

I'm just fine looking after myself, but Mom's got to do her part and pay the bills and give me the twenty bucks a week I need to buy frozen pizzas and bagels and stuff at the convenience store so I don't starve.

The thing is, I got more problems lining up:

The dryer broke, so I got wet clothes hanging up about everywhere I look.

A new kind of bug with lots of legs has been crawling around in the hallway. No, not really crawling—these bugs run. Like they're scared of *me*. On the bright side, I guess I got roommates now, so I don't live all alone anymore.

Some kind of mold is growing on the walls in my bathroom. It's blue. And I'm seriously worried that it might be radioactive.

The damn shampoo bottle in the shower's almost empty. Up until first grade, Mom let me take bubble baths, and they were so much better than showers. Those baths warmed me up inside and out, but even back then, stuff always changed in my life before I was ready for it....

Mom doesn't buy No More Tears shampoo anymore 'cause I know how to keep my eyes shut when I rinse. Plus she told me seven years old is way past time for me to start taking showers 'stead of baths, seeing as only babies take baths... and baths are a big waste of water and take way too much time, anyhow.

Sometimes I miss long, hot soaks in Grandma's white claw-foot bathtub. Sometimes I just plain old miss Grandma, but she's half a world away from New Hampshire, all the way in Rhode Island. And I seriously doubt Mom remembered to give her my new cell phone number, so I'll probably never talk to her again.

Anyhow, the fridge is leaking all over the kitchen floor, and the foul fridge juice that is dripping out of the bottom smells like something died in there.

The yard hasn't been mowed in months, but I got nobody to blame for that but me. So never mind.

And I'm just plain hungry for some real food.

Sometimes when I think back to all of those eggs Travis and Lily threw on Halloween night, I feel almost worse that it was a freaking waste of food than it was an act of vandalism on the Kinkaids' perfect house. I could've made enough omelets to last me weeks with two cartons of eggs.

The bus comes to a stop, and I stand up, and like a zombie, I crash into Joey, who's trying to get off at the same time as me. "Watch yourself, doofus!" I snap, and my voice comes out sounding as mean as Lily's.

His eyes fill up with tears, and I feel like an asshole because the way things are going for me lately isn't Joey's fault. But still I don't tell him I'm sorry.

At least I don't say "Stop bawling, Princess."

17

THE ELECTRICITY isn't on when I get home from school, and I know right away that I'm up shit creek. Got no paddle either. Everything in my fridge and freezer is probably trash by now. And Mom won't be back to put money in the Fabio book until at least the weekend.

I'm going to starve. Or freeze. And I won't be able to call 911 if I fall off the back deck and break my neck because I can't charge my damn cell phone.

It's four o'clock and there's an hour left of daylight, not one spare battery for my flashlight, and zero cash to buy more batteries. I'm about ready to go over to *anybody's* house to get some light and heat—*shit, when did I start thinking like a damned caveman?* The thing is, if I show up at my friends' houses uninvited, grown-ups will start asking questions. And I mean the kind of questions that could get me reported, and then deported from the world I know. Probably sent off to a lousy group home with a bunch of delinquent strangers. This is the very same reason I can't tell my sob story to Ms. Paloma at the end of World Geography class or Jan at the library. Nobody can know I'm all alone without light and heat and enough food, or I'm a goner.

But speaking of cavemen, they depended on fire for light and heat, didn't they? I get up off the pile of blankets on the floor that I never put back in my bedroom since Emily slept over, and I start looking around for a candle and some matches.

"Shit on a shingle." I spit out Mom's favorite expression without even a tiny bit of guilt that I cursed out loud in the house. If I have to live like a freaking pioneer until Mom gets her act together,

I'll swear if I want to. I go down the hall and into Mom's bedroom. She used to like to set a romantic mood with candles when her boyfriends came over. Hopefully she didn't pack those candles up and take them with her when she moved in with Jimmy or Robby or Doug, or whoever the hell she's living with instead of me.

"Bingo!" I shout, even though I'm as alone as ever and no one can hear me, except for maybe those long-legged bugs, if they have ears. On her bedside table are a whole bunch of half-melted candles—most of them are red, and some of them are heart-shaped. *Whatever.* At least I'll be able to see. Sort of.

And another tiny favor, Mom left a book of matches right beside them.

I guess now I can't say she never did anything for me.

I grab a couple of candles and the matches and head back to my nest of blankets in the living room. I set the candles on the coffee table and light them, then head into the kitchen to find something to eat.

After searching through my cabinets, I decide the rest of the peanut butter and half a roll of Ritz Crackers will be dinner. I return to the spot on the living room floor that's sort of morphed into being my bed *and* my kitchen table *and* my desk *and* my couch, and I spread peanut butter on stale crackers with my finger and hope the bugs who live on the hallway floor are looking for something better to eat than what I got.

It hits me that I'm having a pity party here. A big dumb lonely pity party.

Then I hear the sound of knocking on my front door. The first thing that goes through my head is *How on earth did somebody get to the front door?* since the steps fell off months ago. The second thing that comes into my mind makes me choke on my peanut butter cracker.

What if it's a cop or a social worker who's here to pick me up and cart me off to someplace "safe"? If you ask me, what I already know in life is safe, and the unknown is a major gamble.

I cough until the cracker comes up and then stand and look out the living room window to check who's at the front of the house. It's sort of dark, but I can tell the shadowy figure isn't a cop.

I think it might be Joey.

So after I suck the peanut butter off my pointer finger, I jump over the couch, run down the hall, and open the front door. "What're you doing here?" I look down at Joey. I'm not trying to sound mean, but I can't be too friendly either since I got to protect myself. Joey could easily go home and tell his mom his "not so good friend" Eric is up a certain creek without a paddle and needs somebody to step in and help out. And Mrs. Kinkaid is so helpful that she'd get right on the phone to report my sad situation to somebody who would help me right into a group home.

Like Mom always used to say, "The devil you know is better than the devil you don't know." So I'll stick with my lousy life here on Baker Street.

"I wanted to talk to you, so I decided to come over," he replies.

"What on earth do you want to talk to *me* about?" I sound mean again.

"Well, can I come in?"

I don't say yes or no, but I step back, and Joey climbs up into the doorway without any help. Once he gets to his feet, he walks past me and then floats down the hall in his graceful Joey way. It's not long until he's twisting and turning his swan neck this way and that as he studies every dusty corner of the hallway and then the living room.

"Why is it so dark in here? And cold…. It's really cold in here, Eric." When he frowns, I'm surprised because he's not much of a frowner, but when he shivers, I'm not surprised at all, because if you closed your eyes in my living room, you'd think you were in the Polar Ice Cap climate region on the continent of Antarctica. You could probably see your breath if it wasn't so flipping dark.

I haven't got an answer that makes sense other than the truth, so I don't say anything.

"You have no electricity."

I shrug.

"And where's your mother?"

I can see in the slow widening of Joey's eyes that he's putting the last piece into the ugly puzzle that is my life. I don't even bother to shrug this time.

"You're living here alone," he declares when it fully dawns on him.

"And you call yourself a genius, Kinkaid?" He actually never calls *himself* a genius, but whatever. "It wouldn't take a genius to figure that out."

Joey drops down onto his knees on my blanket nest and gawks at the plate of crackers. "Is this your dinner?"

I can't just let him tear my life apart with all of his questions. So I ask my own. "Why did you even come here?"

"Sit with me," he says. This doesn't answer my question, but I drop down cross-legged onto my nest of blankets anyway. "How long have you been living here alone?"

"A while. Maybe a few weeks… or a month, I guess."

In the candlelight, everything about Joey's face looks sort of soft and dreamy. He tilts his head, and all of his golden hair falls into a pile on one shoulder, and his eyes look like they have stars in them. I guess his familiar face in this cold, dark hole looks just a little bit too good to me. "How are you surviving, Eric?"

"It's not that hard, really. Mom leaves me money for food, and I got a cell phone now, so I can call her when I need something." My answer is lame. This whole situation is lame.

"Did you call her to tell her that the electricity has been turned off?"

"Uh-huh. She's on it."

Joey nods like he gets what's going on here, which is weird because it's happening to me, and I don't get it. "I came over to talk to you about how you acted on the bus this morning. I wanted to know why you were mad at me."

I don't even hesitate to apologize—I been feeling guilty all day. "I'm really sorry about that, Joe. I was bent out of shape on account of no electricity and ice-cold water to wash with and, you know, too many worries." I look away from Joey's starry eyes because I'm ashamed. "I took it all out on you."

"I understand, and I'm glad you aren't mad." But Joey doesn't look glad—now *he* looks worried. "How can I help you?"

I want to say "Ask your mother to adopt me," but instead I tell him, "I don't need help. Mom's gonna get the electricity turned back on, and then it'll be fine." I don't know if Joey believes this, because I sure don't.

"If you need anything—like food or a flashlight—I can bring it to you… or maybe I should talk to Mom about this. She has lots of good ideas."

I shake my head. "If a grown-up finds out I'm living alone here, they'll report me to the cops. And then I'll get taken away."

"No, that can't happen," he says quickly. I'm the only human being under the age of forty Joey is *sort of* friends with, so I'm pretty sure he doesn't want to lose me. "I won't tell her."

Joey stands up, and I have to cover my mouth with my hand so I don't beg him to stay for a while longer.

"Mom's going to come looking for me if I don't get home soon, because it's already dark out." He crosses the room and heads for the front door.

"I usually use the back door, Joe. The steps are missing in the front."

"I noticed. But I can jump down." I follow Joey to the door. "I'll ask Mom if you can come to our house for the whole

Thanksgiving weekend. I'll tell her that your mother was invited on a ski vacation and you need a place to stay."

I nod because it sounds better than good, even though Mom wouldn't have a clue what to do with a pair of skis. But at the same time, I hope he knows that even if I stay with him for Thanksgiving, nothing's going to change with us at school because I can't put myself on the radar. And getting in fights at school to defend Joey from dudes like Travis and Miles would put me on the radar for sure. "Thanks."

Joey opens the door when he gets to the end of the hallway. "See you at school tomorrow." He jumps off the edge and disappears into the darkness.

I go back to my dinner, but not my pity party.

18

MRS. KINKAID comes into the living room where Joey and me are lying on the shaggy white rug beside the fireplace. "I finished folding your clean laundry, Eric, and I put it on top of Joey's bureau. And remember, you and your mother are welcome to use our washer and dryer any time you need to until yours is fixed."

"That's real nice, Mrs. Kinkaid."

Mr. Kinkaid is sitting on the couch, listening. "Where did you say your mother is this weekend?"

Joey answers for me. "She went skiing with her cousin in Vermont."

"Why didn't she take you along, son?" he asks, and I make this lame gulping sound.

Again Joey answers. "Eric doesn't know how to ski."

I don't know if Mr. Kinkaid buys our story, but Mrs. Kinkaid says, "You boys should go to bed now. It's late, and we have a long day tomorrow.... Lots of turkey to eat."

I watch as Joey says good night to his parents. He hugs his mother tight and then walks right past his father like he wishes he was the Invisible Man. "Night, Dad."

"Good night, boys."

Thanksgiving is usually a total drag, but this year I'm spending it in a real home with a real family. On the night before Thanksgiving, it smells like heaven at the Kinkaids' house, and it's so warm by the fire—I don't think I could be any happier.

It's not even bugging me that Joey's wearing a girl's pajama set.

AFTER WE brush our teeth, I change into clean sweatpants and a T-shirt from the stack on the dresser, and we get into Joey's bed. It's a huge bed, so it's not too weird, but then, maybe it's still pretty weird. All I know is that nobody at school can ever find out we slept in the same bed together. But just for this weekend, I figure I'll forget all about school and my mom and worrying if the electric bill is going to get paid in December, and I'll pretend this is my family and I belong here.

We lie beside each other in the dark, and I wait for it to get too awkward to fall asleep, and it stays a little bit weird but is mostly nice.

I WAKE up because something is different than usual. Maybe it's that Joey's big bed is softer than my living room floor, or maybe the pillow smells like a meadow of flowers, or maybe… maybe it's because I feel something smooth pressed against my leg. When I wake up a little more, I realize it's Joey's leg in his silky pajama bottoms that's leaning on me. My breathing gets quick, but I don't move away—not even an inch. I like how close he is because I'm lonely right down to my bones.

I put my hand on Joey's side, and he rolls over and looks up at me. His eyes are wide open, and I realize he's every bit as awake as I am. And then he spills his guts, but somehow he does it with a sweet, breathy voice. "I feel like a girl in my mind."

I grit my teeth and swallow hard, hoping it'll stop my messed-up urge to pull Joey into my arms and hug him tight because he feels a lot like a girl in *my* mind too.

"I *am* a girl, Eric." This time her voice isn't so tiny and soft. She just says it.

"I know," I reply. *And I do.* The person beside me is a girl and has been a girl since we were little kids playing at being a prince and princess on Baker Street. Again I swallow, but the urge to hug Joey doesn't go away. "I know you're a girl. I just don't know *how* you can be one."

"It's just the way I'm wired."

It's freaking confusing, but I'm going with it right now. Because sure as shit, I'm lying in bed with a girl and her breathing is going as fast as mine.

Actually the way she's breathing in and out with little choking gasps tells me it might be *best* for her health if I hug her—I sure don't want her to have a heart attack. And as soon as I got her pulled close against me, I squeeze her face between my hands and kiss her. I'm not talking about a kiss on the forehead like she gave me when Sir Eric pleased the princess. I give Joey a *real* kiss on her mouth, and in my mind, when our lips are pressed together, I see a girl—a girl who is somehow also Joey. I don't get it, and right now, I don't really care that I don't get it.

The kiss lasts for at least six, or maybe even seven, seconds. And I don't want to stop, but I think we both need to swallow… and breathe. We move apart, and again I wait for the terrible awkwardness to set in because mostly everybody else in the world would think it was a boy, not a girl I just kissed. But even if they'd think that, it isn't reality, because I know who I just kissed. And it was the smartest, prettiest girl who lives on Baker Street.

We lie on our backs with our shoulders touching, staring into the darkness our eyes got used to a long time ago. There isn't much to say right now.

We did what we did.

"Good night, Eric."

I fall asleep thinking about a day that a beautiful princess told a knight in shining armor that he pleased her.

MR. KINKAID and his brother, Uncle Patrick, lounge on the couch behind us, watching the football game on the widescreen television while Mrs. Kinkaid and her sister-in-law play with Joey's baby cousin, Sarah. I ate so much turkey and stuffing I have to unzip my second baggiest pair of jeans when Joey and me lie down on the fluffy living room rug to take an afternoon nap. My belly gets *that* swollen with food.

I thought it would be weird to be with Joey today, seeing as we kissed like we were madly in love in his bed last night. But we sort of morphed back into just being guy friends when we went downstairs this morning. I can't explain this situation, even though I want to. The best I can do is accept that I know who Joey is inside, but I go with who he wants to show to the world. And I think it's for the best that he shows his boy self to the world. Nobody else besides me, and maybe his mom, would even *sort of* get how it is. Plus letting the girl Joey out in public could be dangerous.

Today I wished a hundred times that we could be friends at school too. My best times are spent with Joey, and maybe school wouldn't bite so much if I could look forward to sitting with him at lunch and saying hi to him out loud in the halls. But when Mom was around, she used to say, "Wishes don't wash dishes, Eric," and I get her meaning now, even though back then I thought she just wanted me to load the dishwasher. Just because I want something, doesn't mean it can actually happen.

As we lie here, I hear Mr. Kinkaid tell his brother, "Joey has no interest in watching the football game. He'd much rather paint his toenails."

The men laugh and then turn their attention to the noisy game on the big TV. The thing is, just like I get my mother's meaning about how I'm not the sharpest tool in the shed, I get Mr. Kinkaid's message about how Joey isn't the kind of son he wants. And I think if he knew what the other boys at school were like, he'd be proud he has a son as kind and good as Joey. Or a daughter.

I glance over at Joey, and he's staring at the ceiling, looking kind of dark and empty like the way he did right before he charged into the pond behind the pump house in October. He must have heard his father's cruel words too. And I'm suddenly furious at Mr. Kinkaid for being so rotten—in fact, I'm so pissed off that my blood starts speeding through my veins making me feel as fuming mad as my neighbor's dog. But I got no right to be mad because I'm just as rotten to Joey at school.

Thinking about all of this stuff makes my belly start talking to me, and it lets me know if I don't let it go, there's going to be trouble. Still the gases trapped in there rumble so loud that Joey hears. When he turns and looks at me with his dark, empty eyes, I make myself burp real loud, and just like I hoped, he can't stop his smile. Then I close my eyes, think about the pumpkin pie Mrs. Kinkaid made for our dessert later on, and go to sleep.

ON THE day after Thanksgiving, Mrs. Kinkaid takes Joey and me to the Sinking Stone Mall because it's Black Friday, and she says the sales on clothes and toys and sneakers are "out of this world." I'm basically broke, though, so big sales make zero difference in my life. And I'm scared to death that we'll run into kids from school, and I'll have to explain what I'm doing hanging out with Princess Josie. But I worry for nothing. We don't run into anybody we know. And since Mom dropped by early this week, I got my Fabio-book food money in my pocket, and I spend a few bucks on shampoo at Target. I pick out No More Tears even though it costs more than some of the other brands.

Saturday is the year's first snowy day, and even though there's no snow on the ground to go sledding in yet, it's super pretty outside. Joey and me play every card game we know at the kitchen table while we eat brownies and drink hot cocoa. I feel like I'm living in a Christmas card at the Kinkaids' house. It's the best day I can remember.

And the best night I ever had is Saturday night. When we go up to his bedroom, Joey kind of morphs back to the other him—the girl Joey. We lie on the big bed, dressed for sleeping with brushed teeth and combed hair, and when she takes my hand in hers, we talk about things I never talked about with anybody before.

"I knew I was a girl even when I was really little," she tells me. "For all my birthdays, Dad bought me trucks and footballs, and I cried because I wanted American Girl Dolls and nail polish."

"Do you think he accepts you the way you are now?"

"No. He still wants me to be a boy, inside and out. And I've tried so hard to be a boy because I hate the way he looks at me, but it doesn't work. I just can't."

I put my best effort into not getting mad again because I don't feel like spending the next three hours suffering with a bellyache, and more, in the bathroom. "What about your mom?"

Joey turns on her side and looks at me. "It doesn't bother her that I'm a girl, but she still worries that my life will be hard if I decide to *live* as the real me."

"She might be right. It would probably mess everything up for you if you started to be a girl at school."

She nods and lifts my hand to her lips. When she uncurls my fingers and places a tiny kiss on my palm, I get prickles all over the insides of both my arms. "Are you ever going to be my friend at school?" Joey asks.

This is the question I been worrying about her asking me all weekend. My answer's going to be lame, but a lie would be even lamer. "You're different from everybody else at school, you know? And I *can't* be too different." I squeeze her hand to let her know that this isn't anything personal against her. "I got to blend in so nobody notices me—it's my only shot at getting through middle school in Wild Acres."

Joey doesn't argue, even though I think maybe she should. Maybe I even want her to. So I find myself explaining even more.

"It's like this: I want to be your friend all the time, Joey, but... I have to go along with the crowd and do what everybody else is doing, so I fit in. Being friends with you at school would make everybody look." I swallow back a major throat lump. "I was thinking that maybe we could be friends when we grow up, you know?" I actually mean this. I hope she can wait to be my friend until my life isn't so out of control.

Joey nods. "I guess so. I'm just glad I've got you as a study buddy, even if we have to keep our friendship a secret."

"I know. Me too." My heart pounds hard, and one more time, I tell her the truth. "My best times have all been with you, ever since we were kids." I lean in and kiss her mouth with a fierceness that surprises me. Like maybe I can tell her "I'm sorry it's got to be this way, but I really *do* like you, and I wish we could be together every day at school" in a kiss. Afterward I slide my hands up and down her arms like I'm trying to keep her warm, even though I don't think she's cold at all.

When I stop rubbing her arms, she leans over and hugs me. We stay like this until we hear a noise—somebody rummaging around in the hall closet just outside Joey's bedroom—and we spring away from each other like we got an electric shock. When the noise stops, and we didn't get caught, we laugh our asses off.

Even if Joey and me are a secret, we got each other's backs. That's what study buddies are for. Everything about life seems better tonight.

19

AT SCHOOL on Monday, Joey is wearing his mom's pink scarf—not a woolly scarf for cold weather, but the silky kind ladies wear to look stylish. It's wrapped around his neck loosely, and the ends are tossed over his shoulders like the wind blew them that way, but it's not windy today. Then there's his headband, his tight black leggings, his furry boots, the lip gloss... and a few squirts of his mom's special perfume. I recognize the smell from when I sat next to her on Thanksgiving Day.

The bullies start in on him the second he steps off the school bus.

"Joey's turning into Josephine—right before our eyes!"

"And our *noses*...."

"Where's your crown, Princess Josie?"

I want to go up to Joey in the main hallway, where he's standing there looking around with a trapped wild animal's eyes, grab him by the shoulders, and ask, "What the heck were you thinking when you got dressed this morning, doofus?" Then I want to snatch one end of the scarf and unwind it from his skinny neck and rub the shine off his lips with the sleeve of my sweatshirt, and say, "You being a girl is supposed to be *our* secret. Are you *trying* to get yourself killed by letting the whole world see it?"

But of course I stand there gawking at him, just like everybody else. And when he tries to catch my eye, probably for a little support, I spin around fast and head to homeroom. I can't watch and I can't help, and I got my own problems to deal with, like the real possibility of a major snowstorm that would make my back deck collapse, leaving me without a decent way to get in and out of my house.

I expect that by lunch his scarf will be history, but Joey's still wearing it when he floats into the cafeteria. He sits in his usual spot, alone as always, but he doesn't eat. He doesn't read. He flops his head down flat on the table, covers it with his arms, and stays that way. He doesn't even move a muscle when kids tug on his scarf and call him names as they pass by. And it's killing me to see this because I know that when Joey got dressed this morning, he was just trying to be who he really is.

My gut is hurting worse than ever, so I can't eat either, which stinks because lunch is my only legit meal of the day, plus it's free. Both of us are being tortured because *he's* trying to be a girl at school. Mom always told me never to air my dirty laundry in public, and now I know what she meant: don't let the outside world see all the crazy shit of your inside world. *And I don't.* But it's exactly what Joey is doing.

I don't know why he can't keep on hiding the way I do.

I sit here staring across the cafeteria at him until the school's guidance counselor, Mr. Weeks, walks over to his lunch table, sits down beside him, talks to him quietly, and convinces Joey to leave with him. Once they're gone, everything settles down in the lunchroom, but I still can't eat. I got a bad feeling in my gut.

I'M KIND of surprised that Joey's in World Geography class, still wearing the stupid pink scarf. I thought maybe he would have been sent home because he was a serious train wreck at lunch. He sits down beside me but doesn't say hi, and neither do I. It's super hard to believe I ate a big turkey dinner with this kid last Thursday and we kissed on his bed *twice*, and now we're sitting here like complete strangers. But this is how it's got to be, and we both know it.

Ms. Paloma steps out from behind her desk and comes to the front of the room. "The study buddy program has been very successful."

Joey and me look at each other—he's still got wild animal eyes. We don't smile.

"And I have some good news for you. For second semester I'm going to let you choose your own study buddies."

We look at each other again, and this time our gazes stick together. And he says one word, real quiet, but I can still hear it. "*Please....*"

"It's you and me, Sinclair!" Travis's voice booms across the aisle—I couldn't ignore it even if I wanted to. "Right? We're gonna be study buddies second semester, right?"

I turn away from Joey to look at him. "I guess so."

"Okay, class, I can see that you want to mill around and decide who you are going to partner with second semester. Remember to choose wisely; your grade depends on a sound decision. You have five minutes to find a new study buddy."

Travis gets up and comes over to our desks. He looks down at Joey and says, "Take a hike, princess. You're in my seat."

For a few seconds, I don't think Joey's going to move. It's like he's waiting for me to do the right thing and tell *Travis* to take a hike because I already have a study buddy who is working well for me, thank you very much. But I can't... or maybe I just plain old *don't*. Finally Joey gets up, grabs his backpack, and heads to the side of the room, where he stands until everybody except him is matched with a partner.

"Now sit down with your new buddy and...." Ms. Paloma notices Joey standing alone by the counter where she displays her globe collection under a rainbow-colored sign that reads *It's a Small World.* She sighs and says, "Since we have an odd number of students, one group will have to be a threesome, like first semester. Which of you would like to have Joey as your *third* study buddy?"

I stare straight ahead. Travis lets out a loud laugh.

"Anybody? Oh dear.... You all realize that Joey would be an asset to any group, don't you?" Ms. Paloma looks around the room for volunteers, but even after she tried her best to sell him, still there are no takers. "Well, then, Joey, see me after class, and we'll decide what to do about this... this *tricky* situation. But for now just sit down at the table in the back." Ms. Paloma clears her throat. "Now class, take out your homework, and let's begin our discussion of South America's topography."

I lean over and pull my world geography notebook out of my backpack. The notes inside are highlighted in lime green from the last time Joey and me studied for a test together. I flip to the terms and definitions that we worked on before I went home yesterday.

And suddenly I feel sick. Real sick. *I think I'm gonna barf.*

I jump up and run from the room so I don't throw up on the floor in front of the whole class. As I sprint toward the bathroom, I'm honestly surprised Joey isn't the one to cut and run after the "find a new study buddy" ordeal.

I spend the rest of the afternoon barfing in the nurse's office.

At the end of the day, when I get up off the cot to go home, I notice somebody brought my backpack to the nurse's office. It's waiting for me by the door. And I know it was Joey who did this. I just don't know why.

I DON'T go to school for the rest of the week. Every morning I get up early so I can call the middle school before the secretaries get to the office to answer the phones. I pretend I'm Mom by making my voice sound high, and I recite my excuse into the answering machine when I hear the beep. "Hello, this is Mandy Sinclair, and I hope you will please excuse my boy Eric from school because he has a seriously nasty stomach flu, and he's barfing like every other minute. Thank you."

I'm not *actually* sick, but nobody questions it because the school nurse saw how sick I was on Monday afternoon, and probably they don't want me to come back and spread a contagious disease around the school. Mom must've forgot about the December electric bill because the electricity in the cottage got turned off again, and it's cold and dark—all I want is to go over to the Kinkaid's house for a real dinner and that warm feeling I get from being close to Joey and his mom.

The feeling like they want me there.

But I messed up everything super royally with Joey in World Geography on Monday by dumping him as my study buddy.

What was I thinking?

Well, that's an easy question to answer. I know exactly what I was thinking: I couldn't *choose* to be study buddies with the only boy at Wild Acres Middle School who wears lip gloss, leggings, and a scarf to school. Everybody would think I'm gay, and then they'd torture me too. And I'd be out on a ledge, alone, with nobody at all—Joey at least has his mom to look out for him. Besides, I don't think I'm gay. I really don't *know* what I am when it comes to Joey. Maybe it doesn't even matter. And I'm not in the mood to figure it out either—I got other stuff to deal with, like not freezing my ass off.

I grab a sweatshirt because I lost track of my winter coat, and before I even put it on, I jump to the ground from the front door of the cottage. Once I throw my sweatshirt on, I drag my bike out of the shrubs and head to the Downtown Diner. Last time we all had detention, Lily told me on the walk home that the management there lets you charge your phone for the price of a small soda. I can't exactly go to the library to charge my cell phone, seeing as I'm not up for a heart-to-heart chat with Jan. So I can't exactly afford *not* to go to the diner for a small ginger ale and electricity to charge my phone. The bonus is light and heat.

20

EARLY MONDAY morning, Travis calls to tell me our bus stop has been changed.

"What?" I ask. "The bus stop isn't in front of the Kinkaids' house anymore?" On the corner of Baker Street, by the Kinkaid's mailbox, has been the Baker Street bus stop since forever, it seems.

"Nope. Something crazy is going on at the Kinkaids' house. Joey hasn't been in school since last Thursday. He probably caught the stomach flu from you." He laughs. "At least I hope so."

"Weird," I say. But it's actually *really* weird because school bus stops only change over the summer, and hardly ever even then. "So where do we catch the bus now?"

"In front of Emily's house. It's only a few minutes more to walk on Baker Street, so it's no big deal."

"Yeah, I guess." I still think it's messed-up.

When I get to Emily's house, the strangeness in the air smacks me hard in the face, and I know something's seriously wrong. There are *parents* at the bus stop, which hasn't happened since the first day of kindergarten—and we're in eighth grade now. *Even Chuckie is here.* And the grown-ups are all leaning in toward each other, talking real quiet while stealing sneaky peeks at us. The kids are clustered at the other side of the driveway, and they're whispering with their heads down but refusing to look at each other.

Since I'm the last one to get to the bus stop, I race right into the middle of the group. I surprise Emily so much that she spins around and stumbles back, and then she gapes at me with somber eyes. I ask in my coolest voice, "What's going on? You guys are acting like somebody died."

Every single kid's head snaps my way at once, and they all gawk at me like I got three heads and they're all wearing bright purple wigs. I know I stuck my foot in it big-time, but I just don't know how. Freaked-out faces with eyes as round as dinner plates, like Mom used to say, back when I had a mom, are all focused square on me. Emily steps forward and puts her hand on my shoulder. Even through my coat, the weight of her hand feels good because I been so lonely in my cold house this week, but the panic in her expression rips the good feeling away.

Plus the pink patches around her eyes scream out "I been bawling all morning!" even if the wetness has dried. She's got the strangest, most haunted look on her face when she says the words I won't ever forget. "Joey... Joey Kinkaid almost died."

"What the—" It's like a bolt of lightning shoots into my body through the top of my head and rips out through my belly, destroying everything in between. It's too hard to steady myself, so I grab at Emily's hand on my shoulder and I cling to it. "Did... d-did he get hit by a car or something?"

Travis is the one to answer. "Word on the street is Joey tried to hang himself in his bedroom closet over the weekend. I wonder if he used his fancy pink scarf to do it." His smile is evil. "If he succeeded, he'd be doing the whole school a huge favor—nobody wants to look at a dude in leggings."

Suddenly everything in front of me is one big blur—the kids, the parents, the sidewalk, Emily's house on Baker Street. Everything. And then my entire world is set on fire. Next thing I know, I'm on top of him.

I somehow got Travis underneath me on the ground, and I'm pounding on him with all my might. My teeth are gritted and my eyes are squinted and my brain is exploding. It flashes in my mind that Mom once said when she got the most pissed off at me possible, she was "seeing red," but I'm *really* seeing red because blood is spurting from out of Travis's nose *and* his top lip.

Within a couple of seconds, somebody strong with huge, rough hands drags me off Travis, but I keep on swinging and yelling and... and crying.

Travis is bawling too. "You're gonna get booted outta school for doin' this to me!" His moaning and whining is like music to my ears. "Dad—go ahead and punch Eric's lights out!"

I wait for Chuckie to slug me hard—I expect it and I want it. I look at him and grin instead of shutting my eyes to get ready for the blow. But nothing happens. Chuckie and Mr. Monterey stare at me with straight-line mouths and hold me back from finishing what I started with Travis.

"I don't care what they do!" I scream in a raspy, high-pitched voice that I never heard come out of my mouth before. And I fight like a raccoon with rabies to get loose from the grown-ups who are holding me back. When I can't get loose, I shake my head and yell, "Let 'em boot me outta school! I don't give a shit!"

All I want is to run away. But I can't go to Joey's house because he tried to kill himself on account of me, and my hands are too bloody to go see Jan at the library—I'd get blood all over the nice hardcover books—and my house is dark and cold and loaded with bugs and mold and that smelly juice leaking out of the fridge.... and I can't get away from the grown-ups anyhow. "Lemme go, you assholes!"

I need to be free of the squeezing arms and the gawking eyes and the pain in my gut that feels like somebody set my belly on fire.

I'm losing it.

When the blackness comes, along with the peace and quiet, there's really nothing I want more.

I'M IN the nurse's office again. This time I'm sort of alone because the curtain's drawn around the cot, but I can hear the low rumble of concerned grown-up voices. I know they're talking about me, and I don't care.

It's all kind of hazy, but from what I remember, when I got to the bus stop, I found out that Joey tried to kill himself; then Travis made a wisecrack about Joey's pink scarf, and I lost it. All hell broke loose in my head, and I snapped like a twig on the pump house path. I beat Travis senseless, even though he's twice my size. Then I mentally exploded, or maybe I just fainted, and Mr. Monterey, who was helping to hold me back from finishing what I started with Travis, seat-belted me in his car and took me to the nurse's office. And here I am.

This is what I *know*, but all I care about is Joey.

Guilt sucks, and I know for a fact that I'm a big part of the reason Joey didn't want to have a tomorrow. It's just all too much—it's way too freaking hard.

And I'm so tired.

One by one, the nurse and the guidance counselor and the vice principal step around the curtain and flash me what I figure are fake smiles. But once they're all in my little hideout from the world, their lips turn down, and they look at me with sad eyes.

I expected angry eyes.

I just beat the living daylights out of another student, and they look sad, not mad.

Something's up—and it's bad. Maybe I'm going to jail.

But I ask them about the only thing that matters. "Is... is J-Joey okay?" I don't usually stutter, but finding out Joey's condition is the only thing that counts at this point. "Are you all friggin' deaf? I asked if Joey Kinkaid's okay!"

The grown-ups don't answer, plus they don't seem to care that I said "friggin'," which isn't any grown-up's favorite word. Both of these things seriously worry me.

"What *happened* to him? You gotta tell me 'cause even if nobody knows it, Joey's my best damn friend!" I don't care if these grown-ups know the truth about Joey and me—I don't care *who* knows! I just need to find out if Joey's okay. "Tell me right now if Joey's all right!"

I can't cool down until I know he isn't dead! I won't!

The nurse sits beside me on the cot and pushes my long hair off my face. My *real* long hair that hasn't been cut in months because I didn't have the extra five bucks for a haircut, and now I kind of like it because it gives me a new place to hide. I slap her hand away.

Vice Principal Eickler steps forward and says, "Eric, we found out what has been going on with you. We know that you're living alone."

"Didn't Mom answer her phone?" I ask, my voice suddenly calm. She's hit a new low in being a mother if she didn't answer a phone call from *her kid's school.* Or maybe she *did* answer but refused to come here and bail me out. Wouldn't surprise me. She pretty much told me that her boyfriend's kids come first.

"We're still trying to locate her. But that's nothing for you to worry about right now," Vice Principal Eickler tells me with a pasted-on smile.

I sit up on the cot and cross my legs. "How much trouble am I in?" I think about how bad I bloodied up Travis's face. And there were plenty of witnesses, so there's no use in trying to deny I did it. I do my best to fake a yawn so they think I'm bored instead of scared, but it's an epic fail because a weird squeak comes out of my mouth.

The guidance counselor, Mr. Weeks, is the one to answer. "Don't worry, son. It's not your fault that your mother abandoned you. That's *her* issue, Eric."

I'm starting to get the picture. These grown-ups aren't as worried about Travis's nose as they are about my home life. "When can I go home?" I ask.

"A social worker is packing up your clothes. You're not going back to Baker Street today," Mr. Weeks replies in his practiced counselor's voice.

This is when I clam up, because according to what I heard from this kid on the soccer team whose cousin got yanked out of his house on account of his folks were dealing drugs, I'm either going to juvie or foster care. But I'm not going home. And whatever I say will probably be held against me in a court of law. Mom used to tell me, if I ever get arrested, to shut up until I have a lawyer beside me, but I guess I didn't listen to her good enough, because I already blabbed.

I flop back on the bed and say the only important thing left. "Just tell Joey I'm sorry."

PART II
River Otters, Science Scholars, and Finally Friends

21

MOM DRIVES me to school on the first day of high school. I'm going to have to take the bus home this afternoon because she'll still be at work. It's okay—I'm cool with that.

She pulls over in the drop-off loop in front of the Wild Acres High School, and I hop out of Mom's new-to-her Honda Accord. "See you tonight," I say, hopefully in an upbeat way, even though I'm not feeling hopeful or upbeat about returning to school in Wild Acres. This is a whole new place—the building isn't familiar, and in lots of ways, I'm a different person.

Home's different too. And setting up a new way of being normal with Mom hasn't been easy.

"Have a good day." Even though it's cloudy, I squint when I bend down to look at Mom through the open passenger door. I'm not used to emotional moments like this with anybody, and squinting makes it easier to take. "I'm glad you're back, Eric."

She looks so young with her brown hair in a high ponytail, wearing her waitress uniform for her job at the Downtown Diner. And the fact is, she *is* young. Mom was just fifteen, a year older than I am right now, when she got pregnant. She decided to keep me and did the best job a sixteen-year-old could do with bringing up a baby.

Things didn't start majorly sucking for me until Grandma went into the old folks' home in Rhode Island at the end of fifth grade. Before that Mom kind of came and went, and Grandma mostly took care of me. I guess this explains a lot about how I ended up in foster care in Plainsfield for the second half of eighth grade and most of summer vacation. Mom had to finish growing up and then prove she had her act together to our social worker.

I didn't get this mature perspective on what went down with Mom and me by watching sappy Lifetime movies or by reading books about teenage challenges from the Young Adult shelf at Wild Acres Public Library. I've been in counseling since the week after I went nuts on Travis Jenkins's face and got shipped off to live with Mrs. Marzetti. In counseling I got clued in on how hard it was for Mom to be a teenage single parent. She said Mom needed to mature and finally put her priorities in order. And I'm cool with Mom now because I think she did it…. I think she grew up while I was gone.

"I'm glad I'm back too, Mom." We wave at each other awkwardly. All in all, this little goodbye is kind of lame, but I focus on the fact that it's also kind of cool. And that it makes Mom smile. Still grinning, she pulls out into the high school's big circle driveway, and I'm alone again.

I'm not all alone out on a ledge anymore, though.

When I look at the stretched-out brick school building, I smile too, even though I'm sort of scared to enter it. I suck in a deep breath, hoping it'll give me the courage I need to move in the direction of the high school, and I run a hand through my freshly cut hair.

And I wonder if the bus stop is still in front of Emily Monterey's house on Baker Street.

I wonder if Emily still lives there.

I wonder if Joey survived eighth grade, though I figure I would have heard about it if he'd succeeded in what he tried.

I wonder if any of the freshmen at the Wild Acres High School will remember me from last year.

I wonder a lot of stuff.

It was my choice to come back to school in Wild Acres, though. Mom even said we could move away and start over somewhere else if I had a problem with going to public school in Wild Acres. Or I could get my high school diploma with an online secondary education program right on our living room couch, but I told her I wanted to come here.

It's cool how Mom is willing to bend over backward for me now. Times have sure changed. I wonder exactly how much the kids at school have changed.

"OMG—is that you, Eric?" One of my questions is answered as soon as I set foot in the front lobby of the building. It looks like Emily still lives in town.

Wild Acres High School, Home of the Fighting River Otters.

"Emily, I was just wondering if you still lived in town," I say.

She walks up to me, and when she's a foot away, sticks her hands on her hips. "*Hello!* I'm not the one who went away, Eric." She smirks in the same bossy way as she did last year, and when I lift up my hand for a high five, she pushes it aside and dives in for a hug. "I really missed you when you left."

"Yeah...." I know her, but I don't *know* her. I can't go there when it comes to explaining my private business yet. "Well, I'm back."

"Do you have your schedule?"

I pull a folded white paper out of the side pocket of the basketball shorts with Hawaiian-looking flowers going down each leg that Mom bought me to match my brand-new bright-yellow *Just Do It* T-shirt. "I got it last week when Mom and me came here to make it official that I was going to be a Fighting River Otter." I hand the paper to her.

Emily laughs as she takes my schedule and looks at it. "We're in freshman Honors Life Science together."

I swallow hard. My last year's environmental education teacher said I should enroll in an advanced science class in high school since I have "such an excellent grasp on the science of living things." Maybe I know a lot about nature from paying attention at summer camp, but I'm not the usual honor student. "Say a prayer for me," I say.

"We can be lab partners, if you want."

I'm seriously thankful I ran into her. "I might hold you to that."

Emily is the same kind person she was when we were kids. She hooks her arm into mine as if nine months hadn't passed and says, "Don't worry, Eric. This is a new school for all of us."

I smile again and mean it more this time. "I feel a little better about being a River Otter already."

Again she laughs and then lets go of my arm. "See you in science."

I wave at her as lamely as I waved at Mom and then head to homeroom. But as I walk through the hallway lined with freshman homerooms, I only recognize half the faces I see. It's hard to believe I was gone less than a year, and I'm completely clueless. I guess a lot of the kids I already know grew up, just like Mom did, so they seem different. One face I recognize, though, belongs to the biggest guy in the whole ninth grade wing. He's easy to see because his head sticks up above everyone else's. And he doesn't miss me either.

"If it isn't the violent attacking psycho of Wild Acres Middle School!" Travis shouts down the hall and then makes the sound of *Jaws* music as I approach him. "Lookie here, everybody— wack-job Eric Sinclair is back!"

Last night Mom and me talked one last time about the day last year I basically pummeled Travis into the ground at the new Baker Street bus stop in front of Emily's house. My counselor, Dr. Rigby, also helped get me ready to see him today. And a few weeks ago, Chuckie, Mrs. Jenkins, and Mom had a meeting with Vice Principal Eickler, Mr. Weeks—the middle school guidance counselor who got moved up to the high school over the summer—and the high school vice principal, Dr. Rosenthal, to prepare for today. According to our detailed plan, I go right up to Travis and hold out my hand.

"Am I gonna need bodyguards, or is this a friendly handshake?" he asks, glancing around to see if we have an audience, which of course we do.

"I just want to say I'm sorry for what I did to you last year." My hand is still sticking out, waiting to be grasped. I figured it'd be trembling when I did this, but it isn't.

"It wasn't all that bad," he says, squeezes my hand way too hard, and then shakes it quickly. "You caught me by surprise, or else I would've taken you down. But man, you totally freaked out that morning. Never saw you that way before, you know?"

"I had a lot going on back then, Travis. I'm sorry you were the one who paid the price." I deliver my memorized lines exactly the way Mom coached me.

"Like I said, it was nothing… but if you try it again, I'm gonna have to pulverize you." His words are tough, but his face is pink. I don't think Chuckie coached him much at all.

"That's fair," I reply. "Well, I better not be late to homeroom on day one." I turn to walk away.

"So, Sinclair, where'd they stick you last year?" His question seems to come from out of nowhere.

"Huh?" I play dumb because I'm not ready to answer this kind of question. What I went through when I left Wild Acres in eighth grade is nobody's business but mine. And now Mom's.

"We never saw or heard from you since the day of your monster meltdown. So where have you been all this time? In juvie?"

"I gotta head out." I'm not going down this road with Travis. I owed him an apology, and I gave it to him. It's a done deal.

I turn around and walk away, this time without doing the lame waving thing.

I'M SURPRISED at how overjoyed I am to see Emily's friendly face in science class. She's like an island in the storm, which is what Mom used to call Grandma before she moved into the old folks' home.

"Over here, Eric!" She flags me down, and I head right to her. "How has your day been so far?" she asks. Again it's as if months apart don't separate us.

"Pretty good. How about yours?" Mom took me to Supercuts last weekend, and I got my shoulder-length hair chopped off, but I still make the hair-flipping motion that's become a habit over the past year. When I lived in the foster home and finished eighth grade in a faraway middle school, I got used to disappearing behind my long hair—it seemed like a safe place to hide. I liked it that I could take the hiding spot with me wherever I went. I hid in my hair at school, at counseling, at the mall, and at the church I attended with Mrs. Marzetti, and I only flipped it off my face when I needed to see math problems on a whiteboard or pick an ice cream flavor from a sign on the wall at the ice cream parlor. Now that it's cut off, I have nothing to hide behind.

Mom says this is a good thing, and I'm doing my best to believe her.

I sit down on the last seat on the edge of the lab table, noticing Emily has no shortage of friends. "It's going great. I think I'm going to run to be a freshman class officer," she tells me. "Either secretary or treasurer."

I nod. "You'd be good at both… or even at being president."
There are a couple of girls on the other side of Emily. I wonder
if one of them wanted to be her lab partner, and she had to tell
them she chose me instead. Like I chose Travis over Joey to be
my study buddy last year in World Geography. And I wonder if
she regrets it the way I did.

"Thanks." Emily turns and taps the blonde girl beside her
on the shoulder. "Shaylee, say hi to Eric. He came back to Wild
Acres."

Instead of looking at me, though, this girl, Shaylee, completely
freezes up. Her skinny shoulders are rigid in her long-sleeved lime-
green jersey.

"You remember Eric, don't you?" Emily asks. The tone of
her voice is weird—maybe even strained—like she's trying to
act chill.

Anyhow, I'm not planning to announce that I don't
remember anybody named Shaylee from Wild Acres Middle
School. So I play it cool. Or at least I play it cool until Shaylee
turns toward me, and I see Joey Kinkaid—a more perfect than
ever version of Joey Kinkaid, that is.

"Hi, Eric. I'm not sure if you remember me…. I'm Shaylee
Kinkaid." She doesn't reach her hand out to shake mine, let alone
stand up to hug me like Emily did. But she looks at me directly
with pretty blue eyes that I know and smiles, exposing braces on
teeth I never noticed were crooked. She adds, "It's nice to have
you back in town."

Mrs. Marzetti had one strict rule for her foster kids: no
social media on her home computer. It was to be used strictly
for homework—not to take painful, and maybe even dangerous,
glimpses into our former lives. The other boys at the foster
home snuck and set up Facebook accounts on friends' laptops
and phones at school, but not me. When I left Wild Acres, I was
gone. I needed to get away from there more than I needed to

know what I was missing, and I never tried to be a Facebook detective and figure out what became of my old friends... or of Joey. Even this summer when I moved home and I knew for a fact I'd be returning to high school here, I never looked on my laptop at anything but YouTube videos and games. And I never asked questions. Part of me desperately wanted to know what had happened over the past year, but most of me was too scared to find out. I felt like a person driving past a car accident—something inside made me want to look, but at the same time, I was terrified to see.

As a result of my pure shock, anybody in the science classroom who happens to be holding a feather could knock me over with it. Lucky for me, nobody's got a feather at the moment. But I realize my mouth's hanging open, and I shut it before I catch a stupid fly, even though I now know the chances of this happening are slight. "Uh... thanks." I'm having a finger-up-my-nose moment, as Mom *never* says to me anymore, and I'm super relieved to be saved by the girl on the other side of Shaylee.

"I'm just like you, Eric," she says. I'm fairly sure I've never met her before. "My name is Kendra, and I went to private school in Beverly through eighth grade, and now I'm here at Wild Acres High School. I'll be attending public school until I go to college because my folks have to save up their money for tuition." She makes an L-shape on her forehead with her fingers. "I'm so glad I met Shaylee and Emily at the beach this summer, or I would have been all alone today."

I nod but am still shell-shocked by Shaylee.

Thankfully the teacher, Mr. Diego, calls our attention to the front of the room.

22

Mom and I haven't eaten frozen pizza *once* since I came home, and we don't stand at the kitchen counter at dinnertime anymore like we used to do either. In fact, while I was gone, she cleaned all the crap off Grandma's old kitchen table. It's round and wooden and none too steady but covered in the flowery tablecloth Mom picked up at a yard sale, it looks perfect in the corner of our kitchen.

"The steps for the front of the house that you built this summer are holding up nicely," Mom says as she serves me a slice of homemade lasagna.

"I'm going to paint them this weekend. What color do you want, Mom?" I like to help out at dinnertime too, so I pour our glasses of milk.

"Hmmm… I'm not sure, but I think something bright and cheery. Maybe we should go to the hardware store and look at the paint colors. How's Friday night for you?"

"Friday night works." Things are so nice at home that sometimes I actually pinch myself on the butt to see if moments like this are real. I almost say, for the hundredth time since I came home last summer, "Who are you, and what have you done with my *real* mother?" I stifle it, which is probably for the best.

Most of Mom is like a different lady from who she was when I got yanked out of here and stuck in Mrs. Marzetti's foster home last year. But some of her good parts that I remember from when I was a little kid came back. Neither one of us are talkers; we'd rather keep our thoughts to ourselves. But Dr.

Rigby told me that if I want it to work out with Mom and me, I need to open up.

Looks like I'm in a thinking mood tonight. I never forgot how it used to be when we lived here with Grandma. Even though we never had too much to say to each other, every once in a while, there were days when it felt like Mom and me were on the same team. And maybe it *was* Grandma's team, but still, I wasn't alone. I guess it seemed sort of like we were brother and sister.

"Remember on the weeknights, me and you used to put away the laundry that Grandma had washed and folded during the day?" I bring this up out of nowhere, and I expect Mom to look at me like I've got three heads wearing party hats, but she doesn't.

"I remember." She doesn't gawk or send me a what-the-hell look, but just smiles. "We also had to clean up the kitchen every night after dinner. And if we forgot to change all the bedsheets on Saturdays, Grandma would go berserk."

I smile too. "She hated it if she had to remind us to change the sheets. She wanted us to be responsible people."

But when Grandma moved into the old folks' home in Rhode Island, everything changed—or maybe it was just Mom who changed. It was like she lost interest in spending any time with me, and she went sort of wild—spending all of her time with one guy and then another.

"I regretted losing you, you know, Eric." The way she's looking at me makes me feel like I'm stark naked. I want to get up and run away. I could jump in my bed and bury my head under the covers like I used to do. But I stay.

"I know that," I reply. After all hell broke loose last year and I was officially no longer her problem, something kind of weird and awesome happened: Mom told my social worker that she wanted me back.

"Almost as soon you were gone, I dumped Robby. He didn't mean so much to me after I lost you." I'm looking at my glass of milk, but I can feel Mom's steady gaze on me.

On our first visit together last spring, Mom told me she missed me when I went to live with Mrs. Marzetti. "I didn't believe you actually missed me the first time you told me." It's kind of a spur-of-the-moment confession. I wasn't planning on *ever* telling her this.

When she reaches across the table and touches my cheek, I have no choice but to look at her. Her eyes are wet just like I figured they'd be. "I made a huge mistake—a bunch of huge mistakes. And I *did* miss you, Eric."

The way I see it, something inside Mom's brain snapped, and she knew she'd screwed up monumentally. Maybe guilt started to eat her alive, which I can relate to. Or maybe she went to visit Grandma at her faraway old folks' home and got an earful. But I really think it suddenly hit her that she'd gone and lost somebody who was part of her—a person she might never find again if she didn't make some major changes, and soon.

"Okay." I don't want to argue about why she got me back. The point is she decided it was time to grow up and be my mother. And she did.

Mom still wears all of the same sweatshirts and jeans as she did before I went to live with Mrs. Marzetti, but she even looks different now. She doesn't have worried lines on her forehead anymore, and the dark, tired circles underneath her eyes are gone too. *This* Mom smiles instead of scowls when she looks at me.

I hope she never changes back into the old Mom.

"You're taking wood shop this year, right? Didn't you tell me you did well in that class at Plainfield Middle School?"

I shake my head a couple times to break out of my thought bubble. "Yeah—I gave you the coatrack I made. Building the coatrack was our final exam, and I got an A." I'm bragging, but it's not a crime when you're bragging to your mom. I swallow a bite of lasagna, which isn't as good as Mrs. Marzetti's, but Mom's just learning to cook. And she has plenty of time to get better at it. *We* have time to get better at this being-a-family thing. "Uh-huh, but they call it Industrial Arts at Wild Acres High School."

"Industrial Arts… sounds complicated." Mom takes a bite of her lasagna. "Needs more oregano, I think."

"It's real good, Mom. I think I'll have seconds after I finish this."

She smiles, and it's sort of smug, like she's proud of herself, and seriously, I'd eat *five* pieces to keep that look on her face. "So did anything interesting happen at school today?"

I drop my fork onto the plate. Literally.

"I'll take that as a yes."

I snatch up my fork like I never dropped it, but we both know I did. The prospect of talking about Shaylee with my mother has me shoveling lasagna into my mouth as fast as I can chew and swallow. But Mom is cool—she doesn't push me to spill my guts. And even though I'm speed-feeding myself lasagna like it's an Olympic sport, I'm still considering my options.

When I left Wild Acres last year, I spent some serious time in counseling. According to Dr. Rigby, it was clear one of my "major challenges" was opening up to people, closely followed by trusting them. And after a while, I came to believe my counselor when she said the only way to stop feeling like I'm stuck alone on a window ledge—naked and terrified—is to let somebody stand there beside me. Right now's the time I have to make a tough decision because the trusting part is risky. But Mom broke her butt to get me back, what with counseling and parenting classes and all. And now I'm going to do what's necessary so I can keep her.

"Do you remember a kid named Joey Kinkaid who I played with in elementary school?" I ask but don't look up from my dinner plate.

"He lived right down the street, didn't he? And… wasn't he the boy you were… defending… when you had the fight with Travis?"

When I lost my mind and pummeled Travis into the ground.

"Yeah," I tell her with a nod. And since there's no simple way to put it, I just say it. "Joey's a girl now." My eyes pop off my slice of lasagna and onto Mom's face.

Right away she looks at me over her plate. Her eyes are wide, but she doesn't drop her fork. "He's what?"

"Well, he isn't *he* anymore." I think, *Not that he ever was*, but I'm pretty sure it's okay to keep this detail to myself. "He's a *she*, and her name is Shaylee. I saw her today in science."

Mom nods, and I know she's putting it all together, so I give her a minute.

"Didn't Joey… um, didn't he try to take his own life at about the same time you… well, you know, when you were removed from here?" The guarded tone in her voice tells me she still feels bad about losing me. Mom's apologized over and over for how she acted, but still, her feeling bad about it kind of makes me feel good.

"Yeah. She's Shaylee now." It's weird how easily Joey has become Shaylee to me. Maybe she was always Shaylee to me.

"You told Dr. Rigby and me that when you beat up Travis Jenkins, you were upset at him for how cruel he'd been to Joey, right?"

"Uh-huh. That's exactly right." Looks like I'm coming clean.

"You must have been pretty good friends with Joey to get that angry."

I shrug. I was actually a pretty lousy friend to Joey.

"Did you do what we talked about—did you say sorry to Travis at school today?"

"Yup. And he took it pretty well."

"Good. I'm proud of you for doing that. I'm sure it wasn't easy." Mom pats her mouth with one of our new red-and-white checkered cloth napkins from a yard sale we went to together on Labor Day weekend. The napkins are faded from being washed a thousand times before we got them, but you still get the "we're on a family picnic" vibe when you wipe your mouth.

On Thanksgiving Day last year, we used cloth napkins at Joey's house, back when Shaylee was Joey. Now we use cloth napkins at our house *every night*. It makes dinner feel special, even if it makes more laundry for Mom.

"I guess you have to figure out how to deal with your feelings for Shaylee." She sends me one of those motherly glances that reminds me of Emily, and I don't look away.

If I were the old Eric from last year, I'm pretty sure I'd mumble a swear word under my breath. And I'd pray she'd mind her own damn business. But I'm in high school now, and I've grown up a lot since I was in middle school. I know Mom is just trying to help. "I guess I have some stuff to think about."

"We all do, Eric. Every day I have to live with my regrets about how I let things slip away with you. And no matter how much I want to, I can't change the past. All I can do is try to come up with ways I can do things better now and in the future." She stands up and takes our plates to the sink, but I don't miss how she blinks away the wetness in her eyes. And I reach back and pinch my butt just to check that this is all real. "Now both of us had better get going on our homework if you want to graduate from high school and I want to earn my GED."

I like it when we do our homework together. Mom makes a decent study buddy too.

23

I'M GETTING into the swing of things at school. There are two guys from Industrial Arts class, Chad and Dewey, I'm starting to hang out with. I remember them from elementary school—we laugh a lot because Chad was in the orange group with me until he got moved into red, and Dewey was in the cursed purple group. Sometimes we say that the three of us cover the rainbow of brain power, but what's interesting is we all turned out to be pretty decent students.

Chad and Dewy are both thinking of attending the Beverly Technical High School instead of continuing on at Wild Acres High School, and I don't think it's a bad idea. Everybody in the freshman class who's interested in the tech is going on a tour at the end of next week, and I'm already excited because Chad said they have a program called Biomedical Technology that sounds sort of science-y and interesting.

Speaking of science, it's my hardest class, which makes complete sense. I'm doing okay, not great, but Mom always tells me how proud she is I challenged myself by trying it. Last night, though, I had some major trouble getting my homework done.

In class today, when we switched papers at our lab table and corrected each other's homework, I was kind of humiliated because Shaylee got my paper. The truth is I had no clue how to answer two-thirds of the questions. So she got a close-up look at my biggest weakness—book smarts.

At the end of class, Shaylee comes over and stands next to my chair while I pack up my stuff. It's like she's waiting for something. I feel sort of overwhelmed by her presence behind me—a little bit because she had to mark almost all of my homework answers wrong and she probably thinks I'm stupid, but mainly because of my lingering guilt over how I treated her last year. I know how she had to live as the gender she was given at birth and as a person who wanted to leave the world forever. I also know *our* history as each other's first kiss. And I can't forget I was about the worst friend she could have ever asked for when she needed one the most. I know I let her down in so many ways. All of this *knowing* makes me feel awkward.

And then there's the fact that now I don't think she's just plain pretty—I think she's the coolest girl in the whole entire school. This complicates things.

"Hi, Eric." She smiles, and I melt a little.

"Hey, Shaylee."

"I hated marking your answers wrong on your homework today."

"Not your fault. I messed up on it big-time." I knock on the side of my head as if it's made of wood.

"Well, if you think back to the beginning of last year, we worked together well as World Geography study buddies, so if you ever want to meet at the Downtown Diner and study together some time, here's my cell phone number." She presses a small piece of paper in my hand. And the strange thing about it is I don't look around to see who caught me taking Shaylee's phone number. I'm just so glad she doesn't hate me, because I hate myself a little bit for how I treated her since the summer before seventh grade.

"Thanks to you I survived World Geography with Ms. Paloma, but I'm not sure how much I helped *you*. So… how about we meet up tonight?" The question pops out of my mouth before I have a chance to choke. "If you can meet me there, we can have dinner, and since my mom works at the

Downtown Diner, she can drive us both home at the end of her shift."

Shaylee looks down at the floor like she's shy, but I don't think she really is. It's adorable how she does it, though, and it brings up prickles on my arms. She says, "Let's meet at six fifteen. Ballet at Miss Jeannie's School of Dance is over at six, and I can walk to the diner after."

This year I'm not playing soccer so I can focus on getting good grades. I can make it to the diner by six fifteen too. I only nod, though, because I'm suddenly tongue-tied.

"See you tonight, Eric." She walks past, and I watch her with a grin.

When she glances back, I wave.

I USED to care about what everybody thought—it was actually *all* I cared about in eighth grade, other than staying alive. And I used to blame this on how I was trying to keep a low profile so nobody found out I was living alone and reported me to the cops. But the truth is: I was afraid of being a social outcast. I was afraid of having nobody in my life I could turn to for a smile. I was scared that in every direction I looked, somebody would scowl and turn away, or laugh at me and flip me the bird, or even slug me. Or maybe just stare at me.

So there it is—*I was scared.*

Then I lost everything I thought mattered.

Living at home: gone in a puff of smoke.

Flying under the radar at school: buh-bye.

Not getting gawked at like I was swimming naked in a giant fishbowl: all over with.

Having a secret friendship with Joey while hiding it from the world: gone, gone, gone.

But I lost more than these things. By turning my back on somebody I really cared about so I could be safe, I lost my friendship with myself. And maybe friendship with yourself is really called self-respect.

I'd kind of like to get my self-respect back.

Mom keeps looking at me—smiling and winking as she waits on customers—all because she knows I'm meeting up with a girl tonight. I fight not to roll my eyes, but it's an epic fail. My eyeballs disappear into the upper recesses of my eye sockets at least ten times as I sit here in the back-corner booth, waiting for Shaylee to show up. But I guess I'll live with Mom's sappy grinning because it's so much better than her not caring.

Thankfully Shaylee comes into the diner before Mom has a chance to wink at me again. Tonight she's dressed for dance class—a light-blue leotard pokes out from under a white Miss Jeannie's School of Dance sweatshirt, and black yoga pants. Her hair is pulled up into a neat bun on the top of her head, and it makes her neck look like a swan's. When she sits down across from me, I start thinking about a certain swan from grade school.

I don't even say hello. "Remember when we were little kids and pretended at recess that you were the Swan Princess?" It's a stupid thing to say, and my cheeks burn.

Shaylee's face turns pink too before she says, "I remember. I was the Swan Princess because a teacher told me I had to be a bird, not a fairy princess."

I nod. "That was a pretty stupid thing for her to say, but you managed to sidestep her rule."

First she smiles, and then she giggles. I actually stop and think that the sight of Shaylee blushing and giggling is cuter than a kitten peeking out of a brown paper bag, which suggests

I have it bad for Shaylee Kinkaid. "Mrs. Robinson was probably trying to help me out, but it wasn't the right way."

"Mrs. Robinson should have left the kids to be kids and play our games how we wanted. I'm still sort of mad about it," I confess. "She made me feel like what we wanted to do was wrong."

"Do you think it was wrong?" Shaylee's looking at me like I know the cure for the common cold, and I want so bad to give her the right answer, but I decide to give her the truth.

I shake my head. "It wasn't wrong at all. And stuff like that must've been hard for you to deal with… you know, with an adult telling you that you couldn't play at being a princess—that you couldn't be who you re." We're supposed to be here to get a bite to eat and talk about science, but we've jumped into talking about the real stuff. Not that science isn't real.

"It's *still* hard for me, Eric." This is the first time since she sat down across from me that Shaylee's gaze slips away from mine. She stares at the basket of rolls Mom brought me when I got here.

I guess there's no better time than right now to admit something that's been weighing on my mind, especially since procrastinating might let me wiggle off the hook. "I used to think you set yourself up for the bad stuff that happened to you at school by choosing to dress like a girl, and so you deserved what you got. I get it now that you were doing what you had to do."

Shaylee stops studying the breadbasket and looks at me again. In her eyes I think I see relief. She knows I understand, or at least, I understand it as well as a person who isn't walking in her shoes can.

There's a lot more to say on the topic, but Mom comes to the table. "Mom, this is my friend, Shaylee. She's helping me study science."

"Hi, Shaylee. Thanks for helping Eric out. Dinner's on me tonight, okay? So I expect both of you to eat as much as you can fit in your bellies." Mom smiles warmly, and I'm proud that she's my mother.

"Thank you very much, Mrs. Sinclair."

"Call me Mandy, okay?" Mom's smile is as pretty as Shaylee's, just in a different way. "What can I get you kids for supper?"

WE EAT as much as we did last year on Thanksgiving Day, but tonight I can't exactly unbutton my jeans to let my belly hang out because we're in public. Plus I think it might be embarrassing to do in front of Shaylee now. When we're finished, we pull our science textbooks out of our backpacks and go over chapter one. She's as good at explaining things now as she was when we were World Geography study buddies.

"Time for a study break?" she asks after we review the textbook for about an hour.

"Definitely. Let's go for a walk." I slide across the maroon pleather seat and out of the booth. "We can leave our stuff here. Mom will watch it."

When we're standing beside the booth, she asks, "Are you sure you want to leave the restaurant with me? We'll be out *in public*—someone might see us together." Her voice sounds sort of angry, and she narrows her eyes when she looks at me. Maybe she's just letting me know she's not going to be hidden again.

"I'm sure." I'm a little mad too, even though I haven't got a right. On second thought I'm pretty sure I'm feeling guilty, not mad. And guilt sucks.

Without another word, we head out of the restaurant. As I pass Mom, I say, "Study break," because she keeps track of where I go now.

It's a warm September night. There are lots of people on the street walking and driving past us, but I couldn't care less about who's looking.

"Why did you pick the name Shaylee?" I ask once we're at the far end of the parking lot. She might tell me it's none of my business, but still I ask because I'm curious.

I wait for her answer as we head for the main road. When we're walking along the sidewalk that leads to a small park, she finally answers. "It has meaning to me."

I want to grab her shoulders and shake the rest of the answer out of her, but I know if she wants to tell me what the meaning is, she will. So I don't ask her again.

After a minute of thinking, she explains. "The name Shaylee…. Shaylee means *fairy princess*—it's an Irish name. It took me a long time to decide on it."

Her answer is kind of perfect. "Are you thumbing your nose at Mrs. Robinson by picking that name?" I think of Mrs. Robinson again. A wave of anger that a grown woman told a small child she couldn't pretend to be a princess at recess rolls over me. I want to shout curses into the night at our second-grade-recess monitor, but I don't swear too much anymore.

"No. I'm just being me." She tilts her head and adds, "But maybe I'm putting it in *everybody's* face a little bit."

"My face included?"

Shaylee shrugs. "Maybe. I can be who I am now, you know."

"Why did you do it?" Another impulsive question pops out of my mouth. The O-shape her mouth makes tells me she knows exactly what I'm asking—*Why did you try to kill yourself last year?* Again she could easily tell me the answer is none of my business.

"Not tonight. I don't want to talk about it tonight." She's not afraid to look at me when she says no.

I'm glad she can be up front with me, so I say, "I get that."

"What about you?"

I expected her to ask about what happened to me. "You mean where was I for the rest of eighth grade?"

"Yeah. I spent some time out of eighth grade too. I was in the hospital for a while after… what happened in December and…." Shaylee seems to change her mind about explaining the details. "But you never came back." She stops walking so she can watch me as I give her my answer. It's almost like she's giving me some kind of a test. This time I'm going to pass it.

"You told me some personal stuff last year… about how you were really a girl. You trusted me, Shaylee, and so…." I sigh and then do the opening-up thing that's so hard but so important too. "After everything happened, I went to the hospital for a few days. I had some health problems from not eating right and having too much stress. You know, belly problems."

Shaylee heads off the path and into the park. I follow her as she makes her way to the swing set, draws back a swing, and leans on it. She's still watching me. "And then?"

"Then my social worker put me into a foster home because, you know, Mom had moved in with her boyfriend, and I was living on my own."

"I remember that."

"And I lived in a foster home in Plainsfield until I finished middle school and for part of the summer." I sit down on the swing beside hers.

"Was it horrible there?" It feels good to see her forehead wrinkle up with worry over me. "I've heard a lot of scary stories about foster care."

"No, not at all." I think about Mrs. Marzetti. She's like an energetic version of Grandma who doesn't live in an old folks' home, but in an old house on a cul-de-sac with plenty of bedrooms. "I didn't mind living at Mrs. Marzetti's house. The food she cooked was super good. There were a couple other kids, though, and sometimes I wanted privacy. It was hard to find a place to be alone because I shared my bedroom with another boy."

"Why did you decide to come back to Wild Acres?"

It's like she's ripping layers off an onion with all of her questions, and soon she'll reach the soft moist skinless center where the heart is—where *my* heart is. But I still answer. "Mom worked hard to fix her life so she could get me back. And she's my mom, you know. I wanted to live with her again."

Shaylee blinks once—just once, like she swallowed everything I said in one big blinking gulp. And then she nods. "Let's swing."

I guess the inquisition is over. I hope I answered the right way, but I answered truthfully, so I guess that's going to have to be good enough.

We spend the next half hour swinging like two kids playing in a park.

24

I'M DOING something tonight most kids my age have done a thousand times before, but I'm doing for the first time since I was a little kid on Baker Street. I'm hanging out with all my friends.

"All my friends...." I say it out loud without even realizing, and Mom turns the radio down in her car.

"What about all your friends, Eric?"

"Uh...." I fight the urge to turn away from her and look out the passenger window and pout, but it's hard. "I was just saying, I have a whole group of friends now." I steal a peek at her, and she's smiling.

"I'm so happy that Emily called and set up this roller-skating date."

"It's not a date, Mom."

"Well, I know it's not *that kind* of date."

"Six of us are going, so it can't be any kind of a date with anybody." If it *were* a date, though, I'd like it to be with Shaylee, not Emily or Kendra.

"That's true. So tell me who's going again."

"Me and Chad and Dewey... and the girls. You know, Emily, Kendra, and Shaylee."

"Hmmm." Mom glances at me again. "It could be a triple date."

I sigh real loud as she pulls the car in front of the Magic Carpet Roller Skating Palace. "It's not a date."

She leans toward me and gives me a hug. "I'll pick you up right here at ten."

I hop out of the car, and even though I'm kind of annoyed by her questions and don't plan on waving at her, I still do. Emily and Shaylee are waiting for me in front of the rink.

"Hi, Eric." Emily steps off the curb and grabs my hand. "You're late. Everybody else is inside."

"Better late than never, right, Shaylee?" I can't look away from her, even though Emily was the one talking to me. She looks so pretty tonight. Pretty in pink, which is also the name of some old-time movie Grandma likes.

"Hello, Eric." Her smile makes my heart flutter.

As we head off in the direction of the booth in front of the roller-skating rink to pay our admission fee, I lean toward Shaylee and say, "I don't have a clue how to roller-skate, you know."

She touches my arm, and I get chills, just like I got that Thanksgiving night when we were so close in Joey's bed. "Don't worry. It's easy."

"I'm hoping my skateboarding experience will save my butt."

Shaylee shakes her head. "I'm not sure if that will help, but I'll show you how to do it."

WITHIN AN hour I've learned that roller-skating isn't easy at all, and it isn't much like skateboarding. Shaylee has scraped me up off the floor at least twenty times, and my only chance at staying on my feet is holding on to her hand. So even though I'm humiliated, I'm happy.

"Hey, man, my butt has suffered enough abuse for the night." Chad has had a hard night too. "And my knees are never gonna be the same."

"You poor babies. How about if I buy you guys a couple orange sodas, and you can get off your feet for a while?" Dewey skates up beside us and does a fancy sideways stop. He's a hockey player, so roller-skating is no problem for him. "We can watch the girls skate. They're pretty impressive."

I nod, probably too eagerly. "That sounds like an excellent plan, but ginger ale for me, if they have it." I let Emily and Shaylee roll me to the snack bar on the edge of the rink. Me and Chad sit down while Dewey goes to the counter to buy us drinks and the girls head off to the rink.

As I sip my soda, I watch the girls roller-skate, which translates into me staring at Shaylee. She's incredibly graceful and skates as smoothly as she walks. I'm so involved in gawking at her I don't even notice when Chad and Dewey pull their chairs up beside mine, put their elbows on the table, rest their chins on their palms, and stare at the girls. "So which one is it?" Chad asks.

It's loud where we're sitting, so I pretend I can't hear. "What?"

"You've got it bad for one of the girls. We're just trying to figure out which one," Dewey yells this time so I can hear him over the music.

"Shut up!" I'm not seriously pissed off, but these guys can't get in the habit of talking this way in public. I'm not ashamed of being into Shaylee. I'm just not up for public rejection, if I can avoid it.

"*I* think it's Shaylee," Chad says with a smirk.

"Me too," Dewey agrees. "Your face turns pink whenever she's around."

"Does it really?" I guess I just gave myself away. "You losers…."

"So you *do* have a thing for Shaylee," Dewy says as if to confirm.

"What if I do?" If one of these guys says anything about Shaylee not being a real girl, I'm afraid of what I'll do. Shaylee's a girl. She's always been a girl.

"Take a chill pill, dude. Shaylee's great. You'll be lucky if she gives you the time of day… you know, as a possible boyfriend."

Chad eases my fears by letting me know he sees Shaylee as the awesome girl she is. I wish everybody felt that way, but I know this isn't how it is in the real world. I've seen the skeptical way some of the other guys at school look at her, like they don't believe she's actually a girl. Not only does it piss me off, but it also worries me. And one time Travis made a remark to me like, "You sure hang out with the princess a lot for a supposed straight dude." He has no idea what he's talking about—Mom would say he's confusing sexuality and gender—but Travis has always been clueless. Sometimes, though, clueless is dangerous.

"You gonna ask her out, Eric?"

I shrug. "Haven't thought about it," I lie. "Well, maybe I will."

The guys laugh but don't push me to declare my love. Pretty soon the girls come back.

"I'm so thirsty, Dewey. Give me the rest of your soda!" Kendra snatches his plastic cup, lifts it to her lips, and sucks it dry.

"I guess I'm gonna have to drink *your* ginger ale, Eric," Emily says sadly, as if she's regretful. "Or your drink, Chad. Is that orange soda I see?"

"Hold on a minute, Em. I'll get everybody a drink." I go over to the snack bar to buy drinks with the extra cash Mom gave me, just so I could do something generous for my friends like this. Luckily I remember to take my skates off first.

Until ten o'clock at night when the skating rink closes, the six of us sit around the sticky table in the snack bar, trading information that doesn't really matter, like what our favorite songs are and places we've always wanted to go on vacation. And when Shaylee laughs so hard she forgets to swallow and orange soda drips out of the corners of her mouth, and then she covers her face with her hands, reality hits me hard. One short year ago, I was living alone in my bug-infested home, wanting nothing more than just to survive, and Shaylee was a couple

136

months away from trying to kill herself. And here we are, chatting about Chance the Rapper and Disney World.

Back then we had no clue life could get better. We had no hope anything would change. I was hungry and alone, and Shaylee was living a lie and being bullied by everybody. We both hit rock bottom. But we survived.

And here we are.

Times change, I guess. Life can get better.

I pass Shaylee a napkin, and she looks at me with the bluest eyes in Wild Acres, and after she pats her lips and chin so they're dry, she smiles.

Here we are.

25

"EMILY AND Kendra are still not here. Let's wait a couple more minutes to go in," I suggest to my friends, who are standing near the water fountain in the high school foyer.

Shaylee smiles at me. I think she knows I'm trying to look out for her.

"Safety in numbers," I say softly and smile back.

Chad steps up and leans his elbow on my shoulder. "I'm in no rush. Hot lunch today is chop suey."

"I love their chop suey—I live for it!" Dewey protests. "And haven't you heard—chop suey waits for no one." He's only kidding, though. Dewey's as thrilled to have a gang of kids to hang out with as the rest of us.

I'm happy to see Shaylee laugh. She's always nervous before we head into the cafeteria. I don't blame her because I still think lunch tables are a little bit like planets at war.

"Hey! We made it!" Kendra yells as she rushes down the hall from the English wing.

"Thanks for waiting for us, you guys!" Emily is right behind her. "We had to talk to Mrs. Leach about a new literature magazine we want to start. We want to call it *The Wild Acres Current* and publish poems and short stories and maybe even some art."

"I'd like to be involved in that," Shaylee offers. "I love to draw."

"Me too," I hear myself say, and I'm not too surprised, which is pretty surprising. "Come on, let's go get something to eat, and you can tell us more about it."

As we head toward the cafeteria, like always, I cross my fingers and hope for the best. It's a habit, I guess, because I know that although some things have changed a lot since I left Wild Acres, others haven't changed at all. And I hate to be a downer, but I don't think these particular things—like assholes being assholes—are going get better anytime soon.

Mom changed, and she's still changing. She's trying hard to be a mother first and everything else second. Shaylee's changed; first of all because she's living her life honestly as Shaylee, not Joey, which took courage. But she's different, more at peace with herself, maybe, and I think it's because she feels right with herself. And lots of kids who used to be bullies don't bother with it anymore. It's like they learned their lessons or lost interest or grew consciences. I've changed too. I open doors—and windows on high ledges—in my life instead of letting them stay closed.

But Travis and Lily—I have a bad feeling they're the same. I just hope they aren't worse than before.

Our new group—Shaylee, Emily, Kendra, Chad, Dewey, and me—always goes into grade nine lunch block together because packed-to-bursting cafeterias are intimidating places. A lot of the worst stuff in schools goes down at lunchtime because there are so many kids in the cafeteria with so few teachers around to supervise. And there's a personality that comes with a crowd—Mom says it's called "herd mentality"—where people are influenced by everybody around them to act in certain ways.

I admire Shaylee for braving the cafeteria every day. It must be terrifying. Almost everybody in the room knows she used to try to live as boy, and some kids probably think she's *still* a boy; people use this kind of knowledge as knives to stab you in the back with.

By now the cafeteria is just about full, and as we cross the front of the room by the trash barrels, it suddenly gets too quiet. I can actually feel the tension sizzling in the air. My eyes are drawn to the middle of the room, where Travis is standing up at the jocks' lunch table.

"Jo-ey! Jo-ey! Jo-ey!" he chants in a booming, husky voice. "Jo-ey! Jo-ey!"

Then my attention is pulled to the other side of the cafeteria, where Lily stands on top of the hot girls' lunch table. In a high-pitched screech, she joins in. "Jo-ey! Jo-ey! Jo-ey!"

Within a few seconds, about a third of the kids in the freshman class have added their voices to the chorus. They stand up, pump their fists in the air, and shout, "Jo-ey! Jo-ey! Jo-ey!"

Each of us in our little group is faced with the fight-or-flight dilemma. I'm a little bit surprised when this concept pops into my mind; I guess I was paying attention in counseling on the day I learned about a body's instinctive response to a threat—get ready to fight or run like hell.

Do I stick with Shaylee and defend her? Or do I ditch her and save face?

And once again I find myself standing on a window ledge beside Shaylee, and this ledge is high enough to be on the side of the Empire State Building. From way up here, one of two things will happen to me: I'll be stared at by everybody as far as the eye can see while I shiver in the wind, or I'll fall 102 stories to my death.

I have another option....

I could climb back in the window where I'd be safe, leaving Shaylee alone on the ledge.

What surprises me most about my new friends, and even more about myself, is it seems like none of us have much of a decision to make. Even though we've only been hanging around together for a few weeks and are not exactly BFFs, we're all more or less decent human beings. We know Shaylee doesn't deserve this treatment, and doing the right thing is more important than covering our butts.

Maybe there's one other thing we could do....

A few teachers rush around the room haphazardly, trying to get the crowd to sit down and shut up. But they aren't doing a thing to help Shaylee. So the five of us glance at each other and make a spur-of-the-moment silent decision. We form a tight circle around Shaylee—who's freaking out with her hands covering her mouth and tears filling her eyes—and we shuffle backward to the wide entrance, managing to get her out of the cafeteria without being further exposed.

Once we're in the foyer, she breaks out from the middle of us and runs to the nurse's office. We stand in the now-empty circle, gawking at each other with round eyes and shocked faces until Dr. Rosenthal comes out of the office and stands in front of us. "What on earth happened in the cafeteria?"

Naturally Emily is the one who steps up to explain. "When we went in to get lunch, a whole bunch of kids stood up and started shouting, 'Jo-ey! Jo-ey!' and shaking their fists at Shaylee."

Our vice principal grimaces. We all cringe.

"Travis Jenkins and Lily Lee should get suspended… 'cause they started it," Dewey adds. "Not that I'm telling you how to do your job, Dr. R."

"Can we go into the nurse's office to check on Shaylee?" I ask.

Dr. Rosenthal is already walking toward the cafeteria. "No. I want you all to go to the conference room in the office.

Mrs. Lamprey will bring you lunch. Please stay there until I return, as I have some questions for you. And please, no texting or calling Shaylee. Give her a chance to get herself together."

We look at each other and then head for the office, but even though I do as I'm told, I'm starting to obsess over Shaylee. I'm worried that she feels so alone she might not want to keep going… in life. Like before.

And maybe this time I helped out when she needed it. But I want to do more.

AT THE end of the day, I take the school bus to the stop in front of the Monterey's house. Emily's not on the bus because she's involved in about every extracurricular activity known to humankind at Wild Acres High School. Instead of heading home, though, I head toward Shaylee's house.

The big yellow house still looks stately and striking, and the yard is just as perfectly mowed and weeded and trimmed as ever. But the awe I used to feel when I looked at it isn't so enormous, because I've learned that there's a lot to be said for cozy cottages as well. I head up the walkway and then the stairs and knock on the gleaming front door.

When Mrs. Kinkaid opens it, her expression reminds me so much of a certain day last year that I gasp. She's been crying and is about as distraught as Shaylee was today in the cafeteria when so many kids were chanting the name of who she used to try to be, hoping to make her question who she is.

"Eric, my goodness!" She rubs her nose. "Shaylee *did* tell me you came back from being away, but I didn't expect to see you here today."

"I came to check on her." I keep it simple.

"Well, wait right here, and I'll go ask her if she wants to see a friend." Mrs. Kinkaid leaves me standing in the doorway. I half expect her to return with a bag of brownies and an excuse like "No, sorry, Shaylee's sleeping." But when she comes back, she says, "Shaylee says that you're welcome to go up to her room."

"Thank you, ma'am." I don't waste a second. I bolt past her and up the stairs to a bedroom I remember very well. The door is closed, but I knock and then open it slowly. "Shaylee, can I come in?"

Shaylee is sitting on a puffy lime-green-and-pink polka-dotted pillow in the window seat, looking out on her backyard. She nods, so I go in and sit down on the matching bedspread. These decorations are new since last time I was here and it was decorated like a boy's bedroom.

"I hate that they did that to you today," I say.

She turns and looks at me. "Don't worry. I was upset, but I live ready for days like this."

I remember the days when I lived ready for bad stuff to happen. "You shouldn't have to."

"Hasn't anyone ever told you that life isn't fair, Eric?" Shaylee sighs like this is hard, cold fact, but I don't think it has to be quite that simple.

"Come sit here." I pat the place beside me on the bed.

Surprisingly she gets right up and comes over to the bed, but she doesn't sit down. She stands in front of me and says, "Last year when you didn't pick me to be your study buddy in Ms. Paloma's class...." Shaylee seems to change her mind about finishing what she was about to say. But then she surprises me by taking a deep breath and starting over. "You weren't the reason for what I did—for how I tried to take my life."

I shake my head because I'm not sure if I heard her right. I always figured it was the cruel way I left her when she needed me most that set her mind onto the path to suicide.

"Maybe what happened in World Geography that day was the final straw, but that's all it was, Eric. The way I am is *my* challenge to deal with." This sounds like the kind of wisdom somebody would pick up in counseling. "And I have future plans—they change sometimes depending on what is thrown at me, but I know who I am. I'm Shaylee Kinkaid and nothing will ever change that."

"I could have made it easier for you last year. A good friend would've let you know that you didn't have to deal with everything on your own," I counter.

"Well, it's not too late to be a good friend to me now."

"I will—I am." And even though I'm not used to spilling my thoughts, I do. "I was worried all day that you'd try *it* again."

Shaylee finally sits down beside me. The warmth of her arm pressed against mine somehow reassures me that things might turn out okay this time. "No, I'm not going to try to kill myself again, Eric. I don't want to die—I just want to live honestly."

"I want that for you too. I can help and so can Emily… and I'm pretty sure that the other kids in our group will help too."

"I want to trust you guys. I really do." When she turns my way, it hits me that in some ways Shaylee and me are the same, both of us trying to believe in people who say they care. Mom would say we are two sides of the same coin. And she'd be right. "See, after what I tried to do in eighth grade, Mom kept me out of school until almost Valentine's Day. She said she wanted to protect me from such a toxic environment until I was feeling stronger. And I started therapy and—"

"You and me both."

"Oh, good. I'm glad I'm not the only one." Shaylee laughs, and it sounds so good that I laugh too. "But there's more I want you to know…. There's the emotional part of my transition that I deal with by seeing my therapist and attending a transgender teens group. But part of my transition is physical, so it involves medical things."

Trying not to be too obvious, I check out her body to see if it looks in any way different from last year. "You still kind of look like a skinny kid, you know." Realizing that came out sounding mean, I clear my throat and then try to fix my words. "What I'm trying to say is that you're not like a… a *super curvy* lady, that's all. And seriously, Shaylee we were about the same height when I left, and I've grown maybe three inches, but you seem… you know, like pretty much the same."

Shaylee tilts her head, and I suspect she's still trying to decide if she can trust me with her most personal secrets. Finally she nods once like she's made up her mind. "I take puberty blockers, Eric. I've been taking them since last winter. They stop puberty so my body doesn't mature in ways that I'm not comfortable with."

"They can do that?"

"Uh-huh. That's why my body hasn't changed much. I want to start taking female hormones soon." She stops for a second and then adds, "But I've always been a girl. I just want to match the outside of me to the inside."

"That makes a lot of sense."

"I think so. And Eric, if I have to finish high school somewhere else—a place where nobody knows that I used to try to live as Joey—I will. But *I* know who I am, and I like being me. I'm never going to try to escape the world again."

"I'm glad I came here today," I blurt out. I'm so relieved she doesn't want to die that I have an urge to hug her, but I'm not sure whether it would be okay, so I hold back. "What's going to happen at school? How are you going to handle what went down in the cafeteria today?"

"My parents have a meeting with the superintendent of the Wild Acres School System and the entire high school administration tomorrow morning. I'm sure Mom will suggest more sensitivity training for the student body, like they did last year, after... after what I did." Shaylee stands up and walks to the window but leans her back on it so she can keep looking at me. "Dad will probably just sit there and shake his head—and be embarrassed that I'm his 'son.'" She makes the air quotes around the world with her fingers because Shaylee is *nobody's* son, and narrows her eyes again, but she can't seem to stay mad. Her eyes fill like they did in the cafeteria, and tears spill over onto her cheeks.

"He still doesn't accept who you are?" I ask, even though I already know the answer.

"I don't think he ever will." She makes this sobbing sound and then covers her face with her hands. Again I want to hug her.

We're quiet for a few minutes, both of us trapped in our own thoughts. Shaylee's most likely wondering why her father won't accept her truth, and I'm just plain furious at everybody who's making her life harder than it has to be.

"Shaylee! Your father's pulling into the driveway!" Mrs. Kinkaid shouts up the stairs.

Shaylee wipes her eyes with the sleeve of her blouse. "You'd better go. Dad is going to want to discuss this."

I get up from the bed, but instead of heading for the door, I turn to face her. And then I bend down to give her a squeeze. I bury my nose in her hair and smile when I realize that it smells as sweet as I thought it would. "Thanks for talking to me about… like, everything."

She hugs me back. "Friendship is a two-way street— you've got to listen, but you also have to tell each other what's going on."

Shaylee's right. I learned the hard way that relationships need at least as much give as take. I don't plan to forget it anytime soon.

We don't stop hugging until we hear the front door open and slam closed.

26

IT TAKES a few days to sort out, but the major instigators of the incident in the cafeteria end up getting in-school suspensions. Word is that Travis, Lily, and a few other key players are spending every minute they're not doing class assignments talking with Mr. Weeks about why they did what they did, how they think it made Shaylee feel, and convincing him they'll avoid doing the same kind of thing in the future. Either they're going to get more sensitive, or they're going to have to fake it very well to satisfy Mr. Weeks, who is as tough as a guidance counselor gets, not to mention satisfying Dr. Rosenthal. And the entire school administration seems to be interpreting the large number of kids who bullied Shaylee as a serious "culture problem" in our high school.

Yesterday the whole student body of Wild Acres High School attended a lecture given by a transgender woman. Darlene Detoni told us how confusing and scary and lonely it was to be a teenager trying her best to live as the gender she was assigned at birth, which wasn't her true gender. While she was talking, I looked around at the faces of the students to see if they were scowling or rolling their eyes or snickering, but they weren't. Most of the kids seemed kind of spellbound by Ms. Detoni, who is now an admissions advisor at a college in Massachusetts and knows how to give a good speech. A few kids wiped their eyes as she explained how isolated she felt, and not just when she was at school with kids who didn't understand her. She told us she felt separated from her own body until she decided to live as the person she really is.

This morning Shaylee got on the bus at the Baker Street bus stop. Travis and Lily won't have bus privileges until their suspensions are over, which is definitely a good thing, but I don't think they would have intimidated Shaylee today because she didn't skulk around like she hoped nobody would notice her. She walked down the street toward Emily's house with her head high. For someone who had been bullied on the last day she was in school, she looked pretty confident.

It seems like it takes forever to be time for science class, which is our only class together. "I seriously missed my science study buddy," I tell her as soon as we're sitting beside each other. "I don't know if my grade can be fixed."

Shaylee smiles. "Well, we'll see what we can do. Want to come over tonight to study?"

"More than you know." When she smiles at me, I melt. I melt a little more each time we're together.

Mr. Diego clears his throat at the front of the room, so we stop the small talk and pay attention. "Before we get into the wonders of meiosis, I'd just like to welcome Shaylee back to our science class. We certainly missed you last week."

Shaylee's whole face turns a color close to magenta, and I wonder if Mr. Diego did the right thing by shining a spotlight on her. But when the kids in the classroom shout out things like "We love you, Shaylee!" and "Super glad you're back!" I decide saying what needs to be said, even when it feels risky, is usually the right way to go.

I EAT dinner with Mom before I head over to Shaylee's house for a serious science tutoring session. Mom is definitely improving in the cooking department. Her meatloaf wasn't half-bad, but I'm not sure she should have microwaved the potatoes. They were sort of chewy.

Next time the potatoes will go into the oven. Mom says we all have to live and learn, and I totally agree.

Like always I admire the stately yellow house from the street before I start up the walkway. But for the first time ever, when I knock, Mrs. Kinkaid doesn't come to the door wearing her heart on her sleeve. In fact, nobody comes to the door. Voices boom inside the house, though, so I crack open the door, figuring I'll call out to whoever is in the next room to let them know I'm here.

What I hear freezes me on the doorstep.

"I don't blame those kids for what they did to you in the cafeteria! Somebody has to remind you of who you are—and that's *Joseph Kinkaid*—a fourteen-year-old *boy*!" He stops for a minute and then seems to think of something else he wants to say. "You sure don't listen to me when *I* tell you."

"Kevin, please!" Mrs. Kinkaid begs. She's close to hysterical.

"You coddle him, Greta, and you always have. Just take a look at him—he's wearing a skirt and a pink sweater. And the boy probably has a bra on, for God's sake!"

"Dad—stop it! Let me go!"

"Kevin, take your hands off her!"

"You aren't going to pretend you're a girl anymore when I'm around! It's over, Joey. No more puberty blockers or girls' clothes or makeup—I'm putting my foot down like I should have done years ago when your mother first let you wear her dress!"

"Dad—let go—no, not my hair!"

Several silent seconds pass, and then Shaylee comes bolting toward the front door. Her sweater is twisted and sags off one shoulder, and stubby twigs of blonde hair that have been pulled out of her neat ponytail stick straight out over her forehead like a visor. And there are black mascara stains under her eyes—evidence she's been crying. Shaylee sees me, and for a second, she stops and covers her face with her hands in an attempt to hide, but then she thinks better of it. She takes a step forward, pulls open the door, pushes past me, and races down the walkway onto the sidewalk.

So I do what I did best when I was a little kid—I chase her. But this time we're not swimming down the sidewalk in our world beneath the sea or flying high in the sky like graceful and important birds. This time Shaylee's running for her life, and I'm just trying to catch up.

She races down the Baker Street sidewalk. For a few seconds, I wonder if she's going to cut over toward the path leading to the pump house pond so she can drown her sorrows, but then I realize it doesn't much matter where she's heading. Wherever she's going, I plan to follow along. Instead of running into the woods, she sprints down Baker Street, and I don't catch up to her until we're close to my house. I grab her arm and shout, "Come into my house and we can talk!"

As she yanks her arm out of my grasp, Shaylee yells back, "Why? What's the point of talking? I can't be who he wants me to be!"

"Let's just talk about it." This time I don't shout, and I don't try to grab her again. *And* I don't have to worry that my house is too much of a disaster for her to see because Mom and me have worked hard to fix it up. Even the long-legged running bugs are gone, and I don't miss them one bit. I head down the dirt driveway toward our cottage. "Come on."

This time Shaylee follows *me*.

MOM IS so cool. She welcomes Shaylee with a smile that's just the right size, pours us each a glass of ginger ale, and disappears into her bedroom so we can talk in private.

"Dad tried to pull my sweater off because it's a girl's sweater, and then he grabbed my hair and tore it out of my ponytail. I ran out the door right after he grabbed the scissors and started to cut the front of my hair off!" She reaches up and tugs on the short blonde strands above her eyes. "He's never going to accept me," she says, picking up one of the checkered napkins on the table and trying to clean off the black stains under her eyes.

"Does he have to accept you? I mean, can't you still be *you* even if your dad refuses to see you as Shaylee?"

Shaylee shrugs and sniffs a few times. She's really upset, and I don't blame her. "I tried to be a boy, Eric. I tried for years, and it didn't work. It just made me want to die." I hate hearing her say that, but it's time for her to be honest with herself, and I think it helps that she can say these truthful things out loud to me. "Being a girl has its challenges at school, and I know I have a tough road ahead of me in lots of ways if I want to transition to be physically female, but it's my only choice if I want to… to live. I have to try to do this." She puts down the napkin, but the black stains under her eyes have dried there. "Eric, I'm *already* a girl. And I've always been a girl. I can't be a boy for anybody."

"I think you have to talk to your mother about all of this, Shaylee."

"But I don't want to be the reason they get a divorce."

"*You* wouldn't be the reason. Your dad's actions would be the reason. Now drink your soda." I sound like somebody's mother. "It'll make you feel better." Ginger ale always used to calm my belly down back when I was scared and alone. I don't need to drink it as much lately because my belly is in much better shape. I just kind of like it now.

We sit at the kitchen table drinking our ginger ale and thinking until Shaylee's cell phone rings. She picks it up and says, "Yes, I'm okay, Mom. I'm at Eric's house." After a brief pause, Shaylee asks, "But are *you* okay?"

As she listens to her mother's reply, Shaylee nods a few times, and then she asks me, "Can I stay here tonight? Mom and Dad need some more time to talk." Her eyes are round and wide and scared.

I nod. "Sure. You can take my bed, and I'll sleep on the couch." I'm not worried because my sheets are always clean these days. It crosses my mind that life has turned around for me and looks a lot brighter than last year at this time. I hope the same can happen for Shaylee.

"Thanks, Eric." After Shaylee tells her mother she's all set for tonight and that she'll stop by in the morning to get ready for school, she ends the call. "Want to study science for a while?"

I realize I'm still wearing my backpack, and so I swing it off my shoulders and lower it to the floor. "If you're up to it."

"I think it'll take my mind off what's going on at home."

"Then let's hit the books." I pull out my textbook and stick it on the table.

We study until Shaylee starts falling asleep in her chair.

27

WHEN WE get to Shaylee's house in the morning, Mr. Kinkaid's truck is gone. I'm sure she notices and that she wonders why he's left for work so early, but she doesn't say anything. We go inside and find Mrs. Kinkaid sitting at the kitchen table, wrapped in her fuzzy light-blue bathrobe and drinking a cup of coffee. As soon as we come through the door, she stands up and rushes toward Shaylee, hugs her, and then pats down the spikes of hair poking straight out over Shaylee's forehead. "I asked your father to leave."

Shaylee starts to cry and exclaims through her tears, "I'm so sorry, Mom!"

"*You* have nothing to be sorry about. *You* aren't why I asked him to leave." Mrs. Kinkaid takes Shaylee's face firmly between her hands. "I'm not happy living with your father. I don't feel that I know him anymore, and I don't want to be married to the man he's become."

"Mom!" Shaylee throws herself into her mother's arms, and I step toward the door, thinking it's time I make my exit.

But Mrs. Kinkaid stops me. "Eric, please don't go. I think Shaylee needs a friend this morning."

I look at Shaylee to make sure it's okay that I stick around.

"Mom's right, Eric. I want you to stay. And I need to go to school—I missed all of last week, and I can't afford to miss any more."

"Okay, dear." Mrs. Kinkaid pats Shaylee on the shoulder. "Why don't you go upstairs and get ready for school? I'll get dressed too. And I'll drive you two there so you're on time."

"I hope I can make my hair look normal." Before Shaylee heads up the stairs, she stops and says softly, "Thanks for chasing me down Baker Street, Eric."

I think, *I'll follow you everywhere*, like I told her once when we were kids. But I just say, "Anytime, Shaylee."

EPILOGUE

WHEN YOU'RE standing on the sidewalk looking up at the big yellow house on Baker Street, it seems like the perfect place for a happily-ever-after. And from the very same perspective, the tiny tired cottage, a ten-minute run down the same road, looks like it's seen plenty of better days and nothing good could ever happen there.

"You can't really tell what's going on inside a place just by judging from the outside," I say for no good reason, other than that it crossed my mind, as we sit on the swings at the little park near the diner. When we hang out at the park, it kind of feels like "our place," and swinging is the best way to kill time until Mom's shift ends.

It's almost as if Shaylee's a mind reader and knows the tiny details of what I'm thinking, but I'm pretty sure that can't happen in real life. "Well, don't be surprised to see a 'For Sale' sign in front of my house later this week. Mom says we have to find a place to live that's smaller and more affordable."

"Maybe you'd be happier living in a tiny beat-up cottage like ours." I'm a little bit in love with our cottage since Mom and I moved back in and the bugs moved out. The new nonleaky refrigerator doesn't hurt either. "You know, my mom says not to judge a book by its cover," I add. I used to do that with people too, but I'm fourteen now and have learned a lot since I was thirteen.

"I think that's good advice," Shaylee replies. I want her to look at me, but she's staring off into the dark.

I'm stuffed from the huge ice cream sundaes we just polished off at the Downtown Diner. Mom drizzled *way* too much hot fudge and butterscotch on our ice cream, but neither of us had any complaints. And I'm happy to be hanging out with Shaylee for the rest of the night, even if we're technically just killing time. Once in a while we put studying aside to just *be* together, like right now. These are the best times. "Don't worry, you'll be okay when you move. If you want, I'll help you set up your bedroom."

"I'd love that." She's quiet for a minute and then says, "Mom told me that when she asked him for a divorce, Dad didn't cry or beg us to stay. He told her she'd better start packing her dishes and looking for a job." I can't tell how she feels about this just by the sound of her voice. But I figure she's hurt and worried and will let me know when she's ready.

"Your mom already has a job—she's an awesome mother." When I stopped by the library last week, Jan told me, sort of in secret, that Mrs. Kinkaid was going to take over for her in the children's room, so I already know the rest of what Shaylee's about to say.

But the way Shaylee looks at me makes me feel like I've got all the answers. "Mom would love to hear you say that because it's exactly how she sees being a parent. She went to college to be a librarian, though, and I think she's excited because the Wild Acres Public Library hired her as the new children's librarian."

I had mixed emotions when I learned Jan got promoted to head librarian, but I think the little kids will love Mrs. Kinkaid since she knows so much about children's books. Lots of our Baker Street adventures were based on the books she read to Shaylee when she was young. So I promised Jan I'd help Mrs. Kinkaid out at the Mom and Tot Playgroup. I'm going to offer to be her assistant on Wednesday afternoons.

"Your mom will be great at that." For a minute I think about the bigger picture of Shaylee's life—beyond her house and her mother's new job. "Are you gonna miss seeing your father almost every day?"

"I hate to say it, but I'm going to miss our big backyard much more than Dad. I've always been nervous around him because he made it clear he didn't approve of me, and lately it's been getting worse."

I wonder if she'll miss all of the good memories we made as kids when we played in her yard, but I stick with the topic of her dad. "If your dad wants to rebuild the relationship with you, he'll have to do what my mother did and start being awesome," I tell her with a nervous laugh because there's nothing funny about her situation.

Like I expected, Shaylee doesn't crack a smile. "I don't know if he's capable of changing." She shrugs and then shivers. "Let's swing."

It's fall now, and as we swing through the chilly night air in the little park downtown, I shiver too. It's time to pack away my cool basketball shorts for the season and pull out my brand-new track pants. Maybe I should start wearing my new zip-up fleece jacket over my sweatshirt too. And Mom's getting me a black North Face parka for Christmas. It's going to cost her a whole week in tips, but she told me it's the warmest kind of coat, and she wants me to have it.

The idea of a new warm coat brings to mind the days when I felt so cold in my own house. I don't think it would've mattered back then if the electricity stayed on to heat the house or if I had a warm North Face parka to sleep in, because I was just so cold and alone in life—right down to my bones. No matter how cold I get now, though, I'm pretty sure I'll never feel that frozen again.

And if I can help it, Shaylee's not going to feel cold and alone either.

We swing up and down at exactly the same time. It's not like we purposely *do anything* to make it happen; it just happens on its own. Shaylee glances at me and finally laughs, then throws her head back like she did when she was a little girl running through the grass. Her long blonde hair flies out behind her, and I remember how she was the perfect Princess of Baker Street.

And when she turns her head to look my way and smiles that princess smile, I think maybe she's still seeing Prince Eric.

MIA KERICK is the mother of four exceptional children—one in law school, another at a dance conservatory, a third studying at Mia's alma mater, Boston College, and her lone son still in high school. She has published more than twenty books of LGBTQ romance when not editing National Honor Society essays, offering opinions on college and law school applications, helping to create dance bios, and reviewing English papers. Her husband of twenty-five years has been told by many that he has the patience of Job, but don't ask Mia about this, as it is a sensitive subject.

Mia focuses her stories on the emotional growth of troubled young people and their relationships. She has a great affinity for the tortured hero. There is, at minimum, one in each book. As a teen, Mia filled spiral-bound notebooks with tales of said tortured heroes (most of whom happened to strongly resemble lead vocalists of 1980s hair bands) and stuffed them under her mattress for safekeeping. She is thankful to Harmony Ink Press for providing her with an alternate place to stash her stories.

Her books have won several Kirkus Recommended Book Reviews, a Best YA Lesbian Rainbow Award, a Reader Views' Book by Book Publicity Literary Award, the Jack Eadon Award for Best Book in Contemporary Drama, an Indie Fab Award, and a Royal Dragonfly Award for Cultural Diversity, among other awards.

Mia Kerick is a social liberal and cheers for each and every victory made in the name of human rights. Her only major regret: never having taken typing or computer class in school, destining her to a life consumed with two-fingered pecking and constant prayer to the Gods of Technology. Contact Mia at miakerick@gmail.com or visit at www.miakerickya.com to see what is going on in Mia's world.

MIA KERICK

MY CRUNCHY LIFE

Every hippie worth his salt fights for a cause, and if sixteen-year-old Kale Oswald wants to call himself a true hippie, he has to do more than look the part. He has to stand for something, so he chooses the local human rights organization... where things don't go as planned.

Julian Mendez is fresh out of the hospital because she thought swallowing a bottle of pills would be easier than admitting to her mother and all the kids at school who she really is—a girl who has been seen as a boy since birth. Her puberty blockers might stop her body from developing into a man's, but it won't make facing her fellow students any easier. Because she plans to move forward with her physical transition—there was never any other choice.

Kale and Julian discover and struggle with their capacity for compassion as they get to know each other through the human rights organization. Sexuality and desire—facets of themselves that are harder to accept—present more of a challenge. But before they can move on—to friendship and maybe more—they'll both have to trust each other enough to be honest.

NOT BROKEN, JUST BENT
MIA KERICK

Braving the start of high school, longtime childhood friends Benjamin Wells and Timmy Norton quickly realize they are entering a whole new world colored by their family responsibilities. Ben is trying to please his strict father; Timmy is taking care of his younger sisters. While their easy camaraderie is still comfortable, Ben notices Timmy growing distant and evasive, but Ben has his own problems. It's easier to let concerns about Timmy's home life slide, especially when Timmy changes directions and starts to get a little too close. Ben doesn't know how to handle the new feelings Timmy's desire for love inspires, and his continuing denial wounds Timmy deeply.

But what Timmy perceives as Ben's greatest betrayal is yet to come, and the fallout threatens to break them apart forever. Over the next four years, the push and pull between them and the outside world twists and tears at Ben and Timmy, and they are haunted by fear and regret. However, sometimes what seems broken is just a little bent, and if they can find forgiveness within themselves, Ben and Timmy may be able to move forward together.

www.armonyinkpress.com

THE RED SHEET

MIA KERICK

Be the change...

One October morning, high school junior Bryan Dennison wakes up a different person—helpful, generous, and chivalrous—a person whose new admirable qualities he doesn't recognize. Stranger still is the urge to tie a red sheet around his neck like a cape.

Bryan soon realizes this compulsion to wear a red cape is accompanied by more unusual behavior. He can't hold back from retrieving kittens from tall trees, helping little old ladies cross busy streets, and defending innocence anywhere he finds it.

Shockingly, at school, he realizes he used to be a bully. He's attracted to the former victim of his bullying, Scott Beckett, though he has no memory of Scott from before "the change." Where he'd been lazy in academics, overly aggressive in sports, and socially insecure, he's a new person. And although he can recall behaving egotistically, he cannot remember his motivations.

Everyone, from his mother to his teachers to his "superjock" former pals, is shocked by his dramatic transformation. However, Scott Beckett is not impressed by Bryan's newfound virtue. And convincing Scott he's genuinely changed and improved, hopefully gaining Scott's trust and maybe even his love, becomes Bryan's obsession.

www.harmonyinkpress.com

MIA KERICK
RAINE O'TIERNEY

SOUND

OF

SILENCE

Renzy Callen exists on the periphery of life, and not just because of the horrific childhood event that robbed him of the ability to speak. Walling himself off from the rest of the world as a means of protection, he occupies his time with art, music, and an obsession with self-help groups—whether he needs them or not. His isolation protects him, and he's immune to drama and emotional games… or so he believes. Everything changes when he meets Seven and Morning Moreaux-Maddox, the wealthy, jet-setting siblings who move from a life of sophistication in Europe to humdrum Redcliff Hills, Missouri.

Both Seven and his sister are impossibly beautiful and elegant, like the stars in magazines and high-fashion models on the runway. When Renzy is pulled into their push-and-pull of affection and rejection, he realizes there is more to both haunted Morning and cold, diamond-sharp Seven than meets the eye.

The three teens embark on a quest to learn the reason behind Renzy's selective mutism, and something more than friendship blossoms between Renzy and Seven. It's during this trip of a lifetime that the three realize the truth they seek might be found in the sound of silence.

www.harmonyinkpress.com

US
THREE

Mia Kerick

One Voice: Book One

In his junior year at a public high school, sweet, bright Casey Minton's biggest worry isn't being gay. Keeping from being too badly bullied by his so-called friends, a group of girls called the Queen Bees, is more pressing. Nate De Marco has no friends, his tough home life having taken its toll on his reputation, but he's determined to get through high school. Zander Zane's story is different: he's popular, a jock. Zander knows he's gay, but fellow students don't, and he'd like to keep it that way.

No one expects much when these three are grouped together for a class project, yet in the process the boys discover each other's talents and traits, and a new bond forms. But what if Nate, Zander, and Casey fall in love—each with the other and all three together? Not only gay but also a threesome, for them high school becomes infinitely more complicated and maybe even dangerous. To survive and keep their love alive, they must find their individual strengths and courage and stand together, honest and united. If they can do that, they might prevail against the Queen Bees and a student body frightened into silence—and even against their own crippling fears.

www.harmonyinkpress.com

A FINE

BROMANCE

CHRISTOPHER
HAWTHORNE MOSS

RUNNING
WITH THE *Pack*

A.M. BURNS
CAITLIN RICCI

Made in the
USA
Middletown, DE